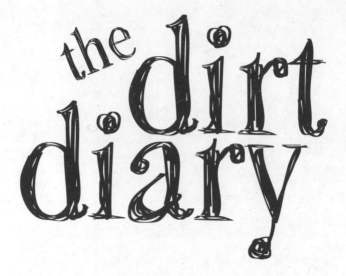

the dirt diary

Anna Staniszewski

sourcebooks
jabberwocky

Published by Sourcebooks Jabberwocky, an imprint of Sourcebooks, Inc.
P.O. Box 4410, Naperville, Illinois 60567-4410
(630) 961-3900
Fax: (630) 961-2168
www.jabberwockykids.com

Library of Congress Cataloging-in-Publication data is on file with the publisher.

Source of Production: Versa Press, East Peoria, Illinois, USA
Date of Production: February 2016
Run Number: 5005991

Printed and bound in the United States of America.
VP 10 9 8 7 6 5

For anyone who's ever had to clean a toilet.

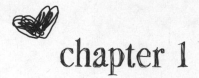

chapter 1

R achel, what are you doing with that toilet brush?"
Mom calls as she comes out of the house with a
mountain of paper towels in her arms.

"Um, practicing?" I say, realizing I've been absently
twirling the brush like a baton. I give it one more dramatic
spin before chucking it into the back of our dented minivan. Really, I was distracted while calculating how much
money I need to earn in the next month ($287.22) to keep
from getting in huge trouble, but that is definitely *not*
something I can admit to Mom.

"All right, are we ready for our first day?" she says as she
slides the minivan door shut. She's grinning so widely that
the skin by her ears is wrinkling.

I nod and try to smile back. I can't believe I actually volun-
teered to give up my Saturdays to inhale bleach, but my efforts
will all be worth it in the end. Fingers, toes, and eyes crossed.

We pull out of the driveway and head toward one of the fancy housing developments across town. To stop my feet from nervously tapping in my sneakers, I focus on my baking plans for the weekend. My mission is to create the ultimate to-die-for brownie. If that doesn't get everyone's attention at the Spring Dance bake sale next month, nothing will.

"I'm so glad you changed your mind about working with me," Mom says, pushing her honey-colored bangs off her forehead. "It'll be nice to spend some time together again."

"Yeah, it'll be fun," I say, my voice high and squeaky. "I looove Windex!" I find myself doing what could be a cheerleading hand motion to show her just how excited I am.

Mom's eyebrows scrunch together, and I tell myself to calm down. Mom miraculously accepted that I'd suddenly changed my whole attitude about her new cleaning business in the span of two days. She *cannot* know the reason why.

"Just remember that we need to make a good impression today, so try to be friendly, all right?" she says, glancing over at me.

Something stabs at the pit of my stomach. "You mean, try to act normal."

Mom sighs. "Rachel, why do you have to be so down on yourself? You're going to be in high school next year. It's time to get some self-confidence." Mom has never had an awkward day in her life, so she thinks being freakishly shy is just something you can switch off like an infomercial.

"I *do* have confidence," I insist. At least, I do in my ability to make an amazing dessert. Dad always says my recipes are a little piece of heaven on a plate. I just hope heavenly is enough to get the most votes at the bake sale this year.

Thinking about Dad makes a familiar ache spread through my chest. Ever since he moved to Florida two months ago—right before Valentine's Day, no less—nothing has felt right. Even Mom, who usually tries to smile and plan her way through every crisis, has been acting totally weird for weeks. That's why I have to make my Get-My-Parents-Back-Together Plan work, even if it means scrubbing every toilet in town. Our family just doesn't make sense without Dad.

A few minutes later, Mom and I pull into a neighborhood of gigantic houses. All the lawns and bushes are blindingly green, even though it's only the end of April. For some reason, I imagine the neon grass tasting like kiwi. Would a kiwi brownie be too weird?

We stop in front of a stone monstrosity with two towers, one on each side of the house. I can almost imagine archers camped out in the towers, on the lookout for intruders. A tiny brook winds around the house and under a bridge at the end of the driveway. That's right: these people actually have a moat.

After I drag myself out of the car, Mom loads me up with some cleaning supplies. I glance down at the mop in my hands. "Mom?" I say, pointing to a label on the end of the handle with the word *mop* helpfully written across it. "Am I going to have to take away your label maker?"

I expect her to at least crack a smile the way she normally does when Dad pokes fun at her Type A personality, but she just grabs the rest of our things and locks the car. I guess now is not the time to bring up how crazy-face Mom has been getting since Dad left. At least she'll have other people's houses to psychotically organize from now on.

When we reach the carved wooden front door, I suddenly feel super self-conscious in my ratty jeans and faded sweatshirt.

"Holy fish tacos, Mom. How do you know these people again?"

"My boss is friends with Mr. Riley. They play golf together."

Wait, Riley? I spot a gold plate by the door with *The Riley Residence* carefully etched across it. My stomach goes cold.

"Do the Rileys have a daughter?" I whisper.

Mom's face lights up. "That's right! I forgot Briana was in your grade."

Oh. My. Goldfish. Briana Riley. I scanned Mom's list of cleaning clients before we left the house. How did I not notice Enemy #1's name on it? I have to get out of here. If Briana sees me like this, it'll be even worse than the Fake Boyfriend Troy fiasco. That whole mess gave Briana enough ammo to use against me for *months*.

But before I can move, the door swings open and a guy about my age smiles back at us.

"Hi there!" Mom says in the chipper voice she uses to answer phones at the law office where she works. "I'm Amanda Lee, and this is my daughter, Rachel. We're here to make your house spotless!" She lets out a little laugh that sounds like a hysterical chipmunk.

I expect the guy to at least raise an eyebrow at the idea of Mom and me being related, since we look nothing alike, but he just says, "I'm Evan Riley. Come on in."

"Is your mother here?" Mom asks as she files into the

foyer. I scurry after her, keeping my eyes down. I just have to get in and out of here without making a fool of myself.

"I'm the only one home," says Evan. "But I think she left a list in the kitchen."

"Great! We'll start there," Mom chirps.

Holy fried onion rings. I can't believe I'm in Briana Riley's house! And this has to be her twin brother. I've heard he goes to a private school for geniuses. So far, he seems a million times nicer than his sister. No one's ever mentioned how cute he is.

The minute the thought goes through my head, my face ignites. Why can't I even think a guy is good-looking without getting embarrassed about it? Of course, Evan isn't as cute as Steve Mueller. No one is. Steve Mueller is the hottest guy in the eighth grade, probably in our whole town. Unfortunately, as of a couple months ago, he's also Briana Riley's boyfriend.

"Rachel, come on," Mom calls, already down the hall.

I realize I'm still standing in the foyer, staring at Evan with my mouth open and practically drooling on myself.

He looks back at me with an uncertain smile. I can't help noticing that his eyes are the same shade of green as his Celtics jersey. "Are you okay?" he asks.

I try to nod and move forward at the same time, but that just makes me lose my balance. I stumble forward and—

Crash!

The mop and broom fly out of my hands and land on the floor, followed by several bouncing rolls of paper towels.

"Booger crap!" I cry, stooping to gather everything up. *Wait, did I just say that out loud?*

"Here, let me help," says Evan. As he kneels beside me, I catch the scents of peppermint and laundry detergent. "Did you just say booger crap?" he adds.

I nod, mortified. Why do Dad's goofy swears always have to pop out of my mouth at the worst times?

But Evan laughs as he gets to his feet, his arms full of paper towels. "That's funny. I think I might have to use that sometime."

I try to say "okay," but for some reason it comes out in slow motion. "Ohhhhkaaay." This is even worse than the one time I tried to talk to Steve Mueller!

Evan just laughs again, in a way that makes me think he isn't laughing *at* me. He grabs one of the rolls of paper towels and balances it on top of his head as he walks alongside me. I can't help smiling.

When we get to the Rileys' kitchen, I almost drop

everything all over again. Every surface gleams like it's covered in nonstick cooking spray. If we had this kind of kitchen at home, I'd be able to bake all the time without Mom complaining that I'm taking up too much space. I mean, they actually have three ovens!

"Thank you, Evan," says Mom, rushing to take the cleaning supplies from him. "We don't want to be in your way, so just pretend we're not here."

He shrugs. "I'll be in my room if you need anything. Don't worry about cleaning in there today." Then he glances at me and flashes a crooked grin. "See you later, Booger Crap."

Great. Perfect. Just the kind of nickname you want a guy calling you.

Ten minutes on the job, and I've already made a total fool out of myself. At this rate I won't even survive until lunch.

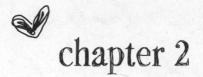

chapter 2

All right, here's the list Mrs. Riley left for us." Mom holds up a pink sheet of paper with writing on both sides. "Do you want to tackle the bedrooms, and I'll clean down here? Then we can both do the bathrooms."

"Sure!" I do my best to match Mom's cheerful tone. If she finds out I'm only working for her to pay back the money I, um, borrowed from my college fund yesterday to buy a plane ticket, she'll... Well, it's better not to think about it. Bottom line: I'm desperate. Maybe I'm kidding myself in thinking I can stop my parents' divorce, but I can't just sit by and let it happen.

After I grab the vacuum and some dusting supplies, I lug everything up the giant staircase and down a never-ending hallway. How many bedrooms does this place have, anyway? At the very end of the hall I find a huge master bedroom that's pretty much spotless, but I vacuum and dust and fluff anyway.

Just as I'm finishing up, my cell phone beeps. It's a text message from my best (and only) friend, Marisol. **Are you surviving?**

Barely, I write back. **We're cleaning the Evil Queen's lair. Can you believe it?**

A minute later my phone beeps again. **What?? Be careful! Don't let that witch eat you!**

I put my phone away, feeling a little better. My fingers curl around one of the brand-new spoon earrings Marisol made me out of blue doll utensils she found at a thrift store. She has a matching pair in red. I suddenly have an awesome image of me and Marisol hunched over bowls of ice cream, furiously swinging our heads back and forth, trying to scoop bites into our mouths with our earrings. I'll have to tell Marisol about it when I see her. She'll probably giggle at my weirdness, but unlike pretty much everyone else at school, she won't call me a freak.

I work my way through the bedrooms until I come to a closed door with faint guitar chords echoing from behind it. This has to be Evan's room. I tiptoe past, afraid my footsteps will embarrass me somehow, and stop at the last bedroom which has a "Briana's Room" sign on the door in loopy purple lettering. I knock gently, just in case, and go in.

Not surprisingly, her room is incredible. It has the exact setup I wanted when I was going through my princess phase in first grade: the canopy bed and the oversized mirror with matching dressing table. Not to mention a ridiculous amount of gold paint.

It feels weird to be inside my worst enemy's bedroom, like I'm wandering through her brain. I realize I'm holding my breath, probably so I don't inhale any of her evil germs.

The only thing out of place in the whole room is a pile of softball gear. As much as I hate Briana, I have to admit she is by far the best eighth-grade pitcher my school has ever seen. Her glove and sneakers and uniform are neatly piled in the corner, next to her walk-in closet.

Holy boiled artichokes, the closet is *huge*. I push the door open all the way and wander through the rows of shirts and skirts and pants. It all smells like lavender and fanciness. Everything is hung up like it's on display in a fashion museum. Even Briana's bras are on hangers! She probably has them specially made for her noticeably full chest, which sprouted the summer before sixth grade (and made her the envy of all the girls).

I can't wait to tell Marisol that I've actually seen Briana's whole wardrobe. She'll probably grill me about every article of clothing.

With a sigh, I grab the vacuum and get back to work. The last thing I need is Briana coming home to find me pawing through her stuff.

When I'm almost done cleaning, I notice a bulletin board covered with photos hanging over Briana's desk. Most of them are of Briana and her best friend, Caitlin Schubert, at a bunch of exotic vacation spots. Even on a tropical beach, Caitlin still looks miserable. She has this attitude like everything is beneath her, and her face is always twisted into a sucking-limes sneer. If Briana is the Evil Queen, then Caitlin is the Wicked Stepsister.

On the edge of the bulletin board I spot a photo of Briana and Steve Mueller that must have been taken before last year's Spring Dance. They weren't dating back then, but they already looked like the perfect couple. She's athletic and gorgeous, and he's like a guy from a Disney Channel movie. Spiky hair. Dark eyes. Adorable dimples. Figures that Prince Charming would fall into the clutches of a wicked queen.

As I stare at the picture, I can't help imagining that I'm the one standing next to Steve, his arm around my waist, my hand resting on top of his. I can almost smell his cologne—it always makes me think of the color blue.

In a trance, I pluck the photo off the bulletin board and press it to my chest, like if I hold it close enough, I can actually be inside it.

And that's when Briana Riley appears in the doorway of her room.

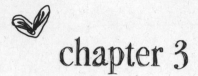

chapter 3

W hat the hell are you doing in here?" Briana demands.
My mind floods with explanations, but I can't
say anything with Briana glaring at me like I'm some kind
of virus. It's like all those times at school when she's practically made me cry in front of everyone.

Briana stomps over to me. "What are you doing with
that?" She snatches the photo away from me with her
perfectly manicured claws. Her eyes swing around the
room and stop on her open closet door. "Were you going
through my *clothes?*"

I think I actually whimper.

"Get out—get out of my room!" She grabs my arm and
starts dragging me toward the doorway.

I can feel the tears stinging at the back of my eyes. Why
do I always turn into a blubbering mess around Briana? I
swear she has a humiliation superpower.

Suddenly, a voice comes from out in the hall: "Relax, Bree." It's Evan. "She's just here cleaning the house with her mom."

Briana's eyes swing back toward me as she finally lets go of my arm. "You're the new cleaning lady?" I can almost see the wheels turning in her head as she processes the information. "That blond woman downstairs is your mom? Are you adopted or something?"

And there it is, the question I know most people who see my mom and me together wonder about, even though none of them are rude enough to ask. Mom is tall and curvy and blond. I'm short and straight and Asian. Half Asian, technically, since Dad's parents are from Korea, but his DNA must have beaten out all of Mom's when I was created.

"No," I half-whisper. "I'm not—"

But Briana doesn't seem to care about my answer. "Well, I hope this job was fun while it lasted," she says as a lip-glossed smile spreads across her face, "because I'm going to get my mother to fire you."

"What? No!" I cry, finally finding my voice. I can't get us fired on the first day. "The photo…it just fell. I was picking it up."

"You're a stalker, and you know it," says Briana, her perfectly straight ponytail swinging with every word.

Evan comes up beside her. "Seriously, Bree. Chill out. I'm sure she wasn't doing anything wrong."

"You don't even know this girl," Briana snaps. "You can't trust anything she says. She made up a fake boyfriend and told everyone about him."

I close my eyes and suck in a deep breath. Why did she have to bring up the Troy thing? Why can't it just die?

"I'm calling Mother right now and telling her to ditch this freak," Briana adds.

"You know that won't work," says Evan. "Mom doesn't have time to find anyone else."

Briana lets out a frustrated puff of air. "Fine," she says, turning to glare at me. "But if anything's missing from my room, I'm calling the police. Got it?"

I nod, wondering if Evan is a lion tamer or something. I've never seen anyone talk sense into Briana before, not even Caitlin Schubert.

"Rachel?" I hear Mom call from down the hall. A second later, she appears in the doorway. "I'm sorry, Briana. Are Rachel and I bothering you?"

Evan jumps in before his sister can say anything. "It's

no problem. She just wasn't expecting anyone to be in her room."

"We'll be here every Saturday at this time," says Mom, chipper as always.

I expect Briana to chew Mom's ear off, but instead she gives her a big, fake smile. I glance over at Evan, wondering if he's using another Jedi mind trick, but he's already slipped back out into the hallway. I try to give him a grateful smile, but I'm not sure if he sees it.

"Rachel, do you want to help me do the bathrooms now?" Mom asks, grabbing the vacuum.

I nod and manage to make my legs start moving again. They feel like two Slinkies.

"Don't forget the trash," Briana says, pointing to a wicker wastebasket overflowing with used tissues. Gross. But I don't want to give Briana the added enjoyment of watching me squirm. I grit my teeth, empty the trash, and rush after Mom.

"See you next Saturday!" Briana calls after me.

The sickly sweet tone in her voice makes my stomach quiver. Suddenly, I understand why she didn't object to me being here every week. Briana might not be able to get me fired, but that doesn't mean she can't find other ways to make my life completely miserable.

chapter 4

The minute Mom and I get back in the car, I grab the list of cleaning clients to make sure there are no more surprises. Most of the names are of people Mom knows through work or the PTA or her book group. After Dad left, she pretty much told everyone in town about her new side business.

I always have the urge to cluck when I see Mom's chicken-scratch handwriting. It doesn't fit her order-obsessed personality at all. The first name she wrote down looks nothing like "Riley." No wonder I didn't catch on. I scan the list again, trying to decipher Mom's hieroglyphics, but don't see any other names I know. Still, I grab my Red Sox cap from the backseat and pull it down low over my face, just in case.

"Are you okay?" Mom asks. "You're really flushed." She gives me a long look like she's trying to laser her way into my brain. "Maybe try some deep, cleansing breaths?"

"How could you take that job knowing the Rileys' daughter went to my school?" I can't help asking, my fake excitement cracking.

Mom blinks at me, clearly surprised. "I didn't realize it would be a problem."

"Of course it's a problem! Imagine there was someone from your grade, and you had to go clean their house. Wouldn't you rather die than do that?"

"I'd be happy to catch up with them," Mom says with a little laugh. "It's been years since I've seen anyone from school."

I shake my head, realizing there's no point in trying to get Mom to understand. Dad would get it right away—he and I have always been a lot alike—but sometimes I wonder how Mom and I are even related. Then again, Dad's the one who up and moved to Florida to start a scuba-diving business after only taking one scuba class in his life. I guess I don't always understand him, either.

After Mom and I drive out of the housing development and turn onto South Street, I hold my breath as we stop at a red light right next to Molly's Cafe. This is the first time I've been by it since Dad left. When I glance over at Mom, she's staring straight ahead like she doesn't even realize where we are. But she's twirling the wedding ring she still wears on her finger. That platinum band is how I know she hasn't given up on Dad either, no matter what she says.

I still can't believe how quickly my family fell apart. One minute, my parents and I were sitting inside Molly's, sipping hot chocolate and waiting for our crepes, and the next minute Dad was announcing he was tired of living in New England and wanted us to move to Florida. Mom begged him to give us time to make the decision as a family, but he said he'd already made up his mind. The next day he quit his job, packed up his stuff, and left. Dad has always been an act-now, think-later kind of person, but he'd never done anything so big before. It was completely nutso.

I hoped he'd at least take me with him, but Dad insisted he couldn't pull me out of school and bring me to a new place while he was trying to set up his business. After he left, Mom announced she couldn't stay married to someone so irresponsible and selfish, especially when he lived in a whole other part of the country. The next day, she put all of Dad's things up in the attic, just like she'd done with all my old toys.

I can't imagine never going to Molly's with my parents again, never eating another banana and Nutella crepe while both of them sit beside me. Those days can't be over; they just can't. That's why I have to fly down to Florida and talk some sense into Dad. Even if it means lying to my parents and dipping into my college fund to get there.

"Rachel, are you coming?" Mom's voice pulls me out of my thoughts. I realize we've already stopped in front of our next house. I take a deep breath and reluctantly follow her.

For the next few hours, all I do is scrub and clean and pretend to be enjoying every minute of it. By the end of the day, I'm dreaming of going home and taking a marathon shower, but we still have one house left to do.

"This one shouldn't take long," Mom says as we drive over to a neighborhood of modest houses. "Ms. Montelle is raising a daughter all by herself and having a hard time staying on top of things, so she could really use our help."

Mom's eyes get misty for a second, and I'm afraid she might start crying. She's been so weirdly unemotional since Dad left, but I guess sometimes even she can't hold it together. Apparently, color-coding our dishes only relieves so much stress.

I try to think of something comforting to say, but all that comes out is: "We should get a puppy."

Mom sighs. "Oh, Rachel."

She pulls the car to a stop next to a medium-sized ranch house with a patchy lawn. When we get to the front door, I hear faint music coming from inside. It takes me less than a second to recognize it as the theme song to *Pastry Wars*. It's my favorite show, all about pastry chefs competing to see who can make the craziest desserts. The best episode ever is the one where a guy makes cannolis that look like snails and puts them on little conveyor belts so they're actually crawling. But he doesn't win because another chef puts firecrackers in her cannolis. The judges always seem to pick people who set things on fire.

A tired-looking woman with dark red hair opens the door. The minute she sees us, a smile lights up her face.

"Thank you so much for coming," she says. "I'm Linda Montelle." She shakes both of our hands like we're important clients. "I'm so embarrassed at how messy this place is, but I work such long hours that I'm always too tired to clean."

"We'll take care of everything," Mom says. I nod for emphasis while peering into the living room and trying to figure out which episode of *Pastry Wars* is on. Someone's curled up on the couch, her face blocked by an oversized pillow.

"My daughter is a little under the weather today," Ms. Montelle says. "I hope it's all right if she stays on the sofa."

"Of course," says Mom. "If she doesn't mind us working around her."

"You don't mind, do you, Caitlin?" Ms. Montelle calls.

"Whatever," a voice replies from the couch. "As long as no one goes in my room." The figure moves, and I catch a glimpse of a girl who looks like she just swallowed a lime. Oh my goldfish. It's Caitlin Schubert, Briana Riley's bosom buddy.

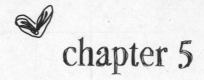

chapter 5

I stare at Caitlin Schubert in disbelief. Is my mom purposely lining up jobs that are going to kill me?

"Honey, come on," Mom calls, waving me into the kitchen. As I follow behind her, I expect Caitlin to give me the stink eye or make some sarcastic comment. But she just keeps watching TV as if she doesn't care we're here. I realize there's a good chance Caitlin hasn't even seen my face. I pull my Red Sox cap down, hoping I can get out of here without being recognized.

"Do you want to start in the bathroom?" Mom asks.

"Sure." I yank on some yellow rubber gloves and rush down the hall.

As I scrub the puke-green toilet, the same type of 1970s beauty that's the crowning jewel of our bathroom at home, I can't wrap my brain around this being Caitlin Schubert's house. Caitlin and Briana have been best friends since elementary school. They've always had the same expensive clothes, the same fancy jewelry, and I know from the photos in Briana's room that they always go on vacation together. But from the looks of her house, Caitlin isn't rich. So how can she afford all those things?

When I'm done in the bathroom, I help Mom finish cleaning the house as fast as I can. The whole time, Ms. Montelle is at her computer scrolling through endless spreadsheets. Whatever her job is, it looks like the brain-mushing kind Dad had before he went wacko and quit.

Mom might complain about her job as a receptionist because it pays next to nothing, but at least she doesn't leave there looking miserable. Judging by the way she's humming to herself while she dusts, she doesn't seem to hate her new side job either.

When the house is almost done, Mom sends me into the living room to start gathering our supplies while she finishes mopping the kitchen. I pull my baseball cap so low over my eyes that I can barely see in front of me and rush past the couch where Caitlin is still curled up under a blanket. As I start packing things up, I see that her eyes are firmly locked on the TV screen. If I can just keep her from noticing me, maybe I'll get away embarrassment-free.

But as I rush past the couch again, my hat keeps me from seeing the edge of the end table. I trip over one of the table legs and sail forward. Of course, all the cleaning supplies spill out of my arms and fall on the floor.

"Gas cap!" I cry as I land on the carpet. Yup, another one of Dad's goofy swears.

This time there's no cute Evan Riley to come to the rescue. Instead, Caitlin swings her eyes away from the TV and gives me a long look. My hat fell off my head when I tripped, so my face is totally exposed. But instead of looking surprised or smug, Caitlin just stares at me for another second before turning back to the TV.

My mind's racing as I scramble to gather up the stuff I dropped. Did Caitlin not recognize me? But even if she thinks I'm someone else, wouldn't she have some reaction to seeing me sprawled on the floor in front of her?

And then it hits me. She *did* recognize me. Maybe she knew who I was when I first walked through the door. But instead of making fun of me or even acknowledging my existence, she decided to ignore me. Because in her book, I might as well be invisible.

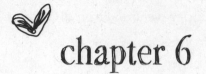

chapter 6

The next day, once my homework is done, Mom lets me go meet Marisol at Second Dressed, a consignment shop on Main Street. I'm not really a big shopper, especially when it comes to digging through used clothes, but Marisol always makes it fun.

"What do you think?" she asks when we're trying stuff on.

I poke my head through the dressing-room curtain and watch her twirl in a '50s-style dress the color of Pepto-Bismol. "Um…" I try to think of something tactful to say. "It's bright."

Marisol laughs, her dark curls bouncing. "I know it's kind of hideous right now, but it has potential."

In the two years we've been friends, I've learned to trust Marisol's fashion sense. On anyone else, her retro garb would look like a costume, but Marisol always manages to pull it off. She claims all it takes is confidence, but I don't think it hurts that she's also gorgeous.

"Let's see yours," she says.

I come out wearing a short cotton dress Marisol picked out for me, tugging it down to make sure it covers my butt. The bright yellow color makes me think of sunlight and buttercups and all sorts of other happy things.

She gasps. "It looks amazing on you!"

I sweep my hair over my forehead to cover my widow's peak—definitely my least-favorite feature—and then glance in the mirror. I have to admit that the dress does look pretty good on me. My normally stick-straight body actually seems to have a little bit of shape to it.

Suddenly, I can picture myself wearing this dress as I pass by Steve Mueller's locker. I can imagine his eyes lighting up when he sees me, just like something out of a teen makeover movie. Of course, more likely, I'd trip over my own feet right in front of him and give him a big flash of my underwear.

"You have to get it!" Marisol says, jumping up and down.

I glance at the price tag. It's only ten dollars, but I know I can't spend a single penny, not when I only have twenty-eight days to save up almost three hundred dollars. And Mom would kill me if she saw me wearing a new dress when all she does is worry about money these days.

Besides, this dress would make people notice me. It's one thing to wish Steve Mueller would give me a second glance, but it's another to have Briana Riley look me over and say something snide like: "Who are you trying to impress? Another fake boyfriend?" That's the last thing I need right now.

"Nah," I say finally. "I think I'll hold off."

"What? But it's perfect on you!"

"It's…it's ripped." I point to a tiny hole in one of the seams.

"That's easy to fix!" Marisol gives me a long look, and then her face softens like she suddenly understands why I'm making excuses. Sometimes it really seems like she can read my mind. "Oh well," she says before ducking back through the flimsy curtain. "So your mom really didn't know you guys were going to Caitlin's house?"

"She swears she didn't," I answer, glad for the change of topic. "Caitlin's mom has a different last name than she does, and I guess Mom thought her daughter was a lot younger than us. Still, can you believe that I have to deal with Briana *and* Caitlin every week?"

I pull off the yellow dress and put it back on the hanger, trying to ignore the disappointment poking at my ribs. Maybe one day I'll come back to get the dress, if it's still here.

"I can't believe Briana brought the Troy thing up again," says Marisol. "You'd think she'd finally move on."

"If she moves on, it'll only be because I've given her something else to make fun of me about."

Who knows why I ever thought inventing a fake boyfriend was a good idea. The plan was for Marisol to send me a couple texts from Fake Boyfriend Troy so we could ooh and ahh over them when Steve Mueller was nearby. If he saw that another guy was interested in me, maybe he'd notice me too. Well, Steve didn't notice anything, but because we made such a big deal about those two text messages, Briana and Caitlin did.

I'm not sure what tipped them off, but after a couple weeks of Fake Troy messages, Briana stole Marisol's phone during homeroom and got all the evidence she needed. Briana told everyone, and I've been the butt of jokes ever since. Figures that when the popular girls finally learned my name, it was only so they could make fun of me.

"Just think," says Marisol as I come out of the dressing room. "In a few months we'll be in high school, and after that it's only four more years until we never have to see Briana or Caitlin again."

I groan. Marisol is convinced that one day I'll be a

famous pastry chef and she'll be a successful fashion designer, and then all the people who made fun of us will regret it. I guess I'm not as patient as Marisol. I want to stop being a loser *now*.

"I can't think that far ahead," I say. "Don't forget. I might not even be alive in a few weeks."

"Your mom won't actually kill you if she finds out about the college money." Marisol comes out in a black kimono and raises her eyebrows at me. "Right?"

"No, she'll definitely kill me." It's not just the money that will get to her. The one time I brought up going to visit Dad, Mom lectured me for an hour on not putting my faith in people who aren't dependable. "Don't worry," I add. "I promise she won't know you helped me."

Marisol nods, but I can tell by the way she's chewing on the inside of her lip that she's nervous. She didn't want to use her only-for-emergencies credit card to buy a plane ticket a few nights ago, but I begged until she finally caved. Since I paid her right back with money from my college fund, her parents will probably never know. I'm the only one in danger of infanticide if my mom checks the account balance in a few weeks (like she does at the same time every month) and sees it's gone down instead of up.

Okay, so Mom might not actually murder me, but she loves coming up with cruel and unusual punishments. One time in fifth grade, after I had accidentally broken the TV and tried to hot-glue it back together, she made me visit a nursing home every weekend for a month to help the old people. To this day, I have nightmares about massaging smelly, wrinkled feet.

"I still think you should just come clean," says Marisol. "Even if you do repay the money, how will you explain to your mom that you're going down to Florida during summer vacation?"

"I don't know," I admit. Okay, so my plan isn't perfect. "I'll figure something out."

Marisol shakes her head, her long earrings jingling. "You know what I think about lying. It always leads to trouble."

"Well, not everyone can be honest about everything like you are." Marisol has three older brothers who are always brutally honest. That's probably why she doesn't care what people think of her, because she expects everyone to have an opinion. I can't imagine not caring how other people see me.

I grab a pair of purple-tinted glasses that make everything in the store look grape-flavored. "Besides," I add. "This is a special situation. I'm only lying because I have to."

"It's just…" Marisol starts chewing on her lip again. "Don't take this the wrong way, but what if your parents split up for a reason?"

The glasses fall out of my hand. "My dad's weird midlife crisis is the reason. My parents were fine before he left. They never argued or anything, and their personalities totally balanced each other out. That's why they're meant to be together. If I can just get my dad to come back and apologize to her, I know they can patch things up."

"I guess you know them better than anyone." Marisol shrugs. Then she turns to me, a mischievous grin on her face. "So, you know what time it is?"

I can't help smiling, even though I feel a little sick to my stomach. "Ugly montage time?"

"That's right!" she says before rushing off to grab some hideous clothes for us to parade around in like people do in movies. I follow after her, trying to push down the stinging feeling in my chest.

It hurts that Marisol doesn't believe me about my parents being meant for each other. But I'll just have to prove her wrong.

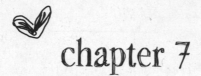

chapter 7

That night, Mom and I sit at the kitchen table eating leftover spinach-and-artichoke casserole. As usual, we barely have anything to say to each other. I try to avoid glancing in the direction of the dining room where we used to eat dinner when Dad was still here. He always had an endless supply of silly jokes to liven things up.

I can almost hear him saying: "Two sausages are in a frying pan. One turns to the other and says, 'OMG, it's hot in here!'" Then Dad would wait for me to say the punch line: "OMG! A talking sausage!" Then we'd giggle like we'd been dosed with laughing gas.

"How's school going?" Mom asks, breaking the silence. It figures she'd try to get me to open up with a generic question. Sometimes it seems like she has no idea how to talk to me.

"Fine." Of course, that's not true at all, but I'm not

about to tell Mom that Briana and her friends have been making my life miserable all year. Mom is the type of person who can't just let a problem go unsolved. That's how I got stuck apologizing to Brett Stevens in the third grade for throwing an eraser at him, even though *he* was the one who threatened to wipe snot in my hair.

The oven timer goes off, and I jump up to pull out the latest batch of brownies. The kitchen fills with the scents of warm chocolate and coconut.

"Is that a new recipe?" Mom asks.

"I was in the mood for coconut." Thinking about Florida so much has made me crave tropical flavors. But now that I'm looking at the coconut creations, they just make me miss my dad even more.

I take out my notebook and jot down the proportions I used, feeling like a scientist. Dad's the one who gave me the idea of keeping a cooking journal, and he even bought me this special notebook for it. After a while I started pasting in photos and recipes to help me keep track of everything. I tried showing Mom the journal once to prove to her how serious I am about cooking, but she just commented on how it was a miracle I could find anything in my chaotic collection of recipes.

As I put the brownies out on the counter to cool, I catch Mom staring at me with her lips pursed into a tight line.

"I'm not crazy about how much time you've been spending baking," she says. "I know you want to win top dessert at the sale this year, but that can't be at the expense of your grades."

"I'm doing fine." I've never been a straight-A student, but I've always done okay in my classes. Maybe I'm not going to go to Harvard one day, but as long as I get into culinary school, that's all I care about.

Besides, the bake sale is a lot more important than Mom realizes. Whoever gets the most votes for their dessert wins a hundred-dollar cash prize. That money will go a long way toward paying back the amount I—let's face it—stole from my college fund. There is no way in Hellmann's I'm coming in second place behind Angela Bareli again this year.

"It's just…" Mom sighs. "I don't want you to jeopardize your future because of a lack of focus."

I can't believe it. We've had this conversation dozens of times, but Mom acts like she has selective amnesia whenever the topic comes up. "I *am* focused! Cooking is what I want to do. Why can't you accept that?"

Mom folds her paper napkin into a tight square. "You're

barely fourteen. How can you know what you want to do with your life? You might change your mind."

"I won't." I grab my dinner plate and stomp over to the sink.

Why doesn't Mom get it? I mean, I literally have mornings when I wake up still smelling the meals I was cooking in my dreams. Isn't that a big sign that I'm meant to be a chef one day?

Mom seems to accept that our conversation is over as she brings me her dirty plate and then goes to add up our cleaning earnings from yesterday. I try to patiently wash the dishes, but I'm dying to find out how much I made. The amount I still need to put back into my college fund ($287.22) keeps bouncing around in my brain.

When the dishes are done, I have to stop myself from chucking the sponge next to the sink like I normally do. Instead, I carefully put it back in the brand-new wire basket marked "sponge." Mom has really started scaring me with her mega-organizing act. I know it's probably some weird attempt to get things under control when her life is falling apart, but I'm not sure how much longer I can put up with it.

I dry my hands and glob on some moisturizer. (Ugh, if my hands are so chapped after only one day of hard labor, what will they be like after a month?) Then I cut the coconut brownies into squares and take a little nibble of a corner. The rush of flavors is amazing, but I think I might have overdone it with the coconut. I guess next time I'm thinking of Florida, I'll try to keep the exotic flavors to a minimum.

"Okay," Mom says finally, waving me over to the table. "This is for you." She hands me a twenty-dollar bill.

"That's it?" I spent an entire day scrubbing, and that's all I have to show for it? That means instead of having $13.78 in the old peanut butter jar under my bed, I'll now have $33.78. At this rate, I won't be able to put the money back into my college account until I'm actually *in* college.

"I'm afraid that's all I can give you right now," says Mom. "I know it's not fair, but I need the rest of it for bills." She sighs and pushes her bangs off her forehead, but they fall right back into her eyes. "I just hope it's enough."

Mom is usually obnoxiously optimistic, but when it comes to money, she's always been really serious. Even before Dad left, things were tight.

"We won't..." I don't want to say it, but I have to know. "You said there was a chance we might have to sell the house."

Mom nods slowly, and I suddenly notice the dark circles under her eyes. "There is. My job at the office barely covers the mortgage. If this cleaning business doesn't go well, I don't think we'll be able to keep the house."

My parents bought our small house when I was three years old. I don't remember ever living anywhere else. How can we just leave it behind?

This is all Dad's fault. Before he quit his job, we were okay. And now he's broke and we're barely getting by, all because he decided diving with tropical fish is more exciting than being with us. I want to hate him, and I guess part of me does, but mostly I just want him to realize he's made a huge mistake and come home.

"Nothing's decided yet," Mom adds. "For now, we just have to do the best we can and save up every penny." She glances at the twenty she gave me, and I know she wants me to give it back to her so she can save it too. But I pretend I don't see her expectant look and slip the money in my pocket.

Yes, it makes me feel like a jerk, but it'll be worth it when I go down to Florida and convince Dad to come back. I haven't been able to talk sense into him over the phone, but I'm sure that when he sees me again, he'll change his mind. Once he's home, we'll be able to stay in our house and not have to worry anymore. Then my family, and my life, will go back to normal.

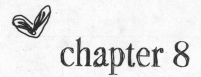

chapter 8

On the way to school Monday morning, I sit in the front of the bus dreading seeing Briana and Caitlin after Saturday's humiliation. I keep replaying the time I spent in their houses over and over, like an endless loop. I wish more than anything Dad was still around so I could tell him about everything, but it feels like he's in a different universe now.

Finally, when I can't take it anymore, I pull out a pen and my cooking journal and turn to the last page. If I can't tell Dad about what's been going on, at least I can write it down in the notebook he gave me.

Dirt Diary, my fingers write down before I really know what I'm doing.

I stare at the words for a minute before leaning forward and scribbling again. I start by describing Briana's room, her golden furniture, her amazing wardrobe, and (okay, fine) her adorable brother. Then I jot down some things I noticed at the other houses we cleaned: Mrs. Foster's enormous collection of garden gnomes (creepy) and Mr. Eklund's habit of leaving dirty socks all over the house (gross). When I start writing about Caitlin's house, I describe the zombielike way she was watching TV and her family's surprising lack of money.

When I'm done, my brain feels a little lighter. After dealing with so much stuff in one day, I guess I needed to get it out and organize it somehow. Oh my goldfish. I hope I'm not turning Type A like my mom.

With that terrifying thought in my head, I get off the bus and head to homeroom. Not surprisingly, Briana's on me the minute I sit down in my seat.

"Hey, Rachel," she calls across the room. "My desk is really dirty. Can you come here and clean it for me?"

Saying anything back will just make things worse, so I stab my pencil into the cover of my math notebook, imagining it's Briana's forehead. Being around her always brings out my homicidal tendencies.

I used to think mean girls only existed in movies, but that was before I met Briana. The worst part is, she isn't just popular and pretty. She's also smart and talented. And the devil.

"Leave her alone, Briana," says Marisol. Which of course doesn't help anything, but I still love her for standing up for me.

"Shut up, Parasol," says Briana. "What are you even wearing? Are you like a housewife or something?"

Marisol just rolls her eyes and smoothes down the skirt of her new pink dress. She's worked her magic yet again by sewing dozens of delicate lace flowers along the hem and neckline of the dress, making it look soft and pretty instead of crazy and bright.

Of course, Briana isn't done. "Hey, Caitlin, did I tell you?" Her voice is on high volume even though Caitlin is at the desk next to hers. "Rachel Lee is my new maid."

A few desks over, Angela Bareli giggles, kissing up like she always does around the popular kids. Angela is Marisol's next-door neighbor, but Marisol and I usually avoid her since all she does is gossip. The fact that she got the most votes at last year's Spring Dance bake sale doesn't make me like her any more.

"Caitlin, if you want, I can loan Rachel to you," Briana goes on. "I hear she's good at scrubbing floors. She probably licks them clean."

The pencil in my hands snaps in half.

I expect Caitlin to laugh and say she doesn't need to borrow me because I'm her new maid too, but she just smirks and turns back to an art book she's reading. I can't believe she'd pass up a chance to make fun of me. Back when the Fake Boyfriend Troy thing first started, Caitlin was always there laughing right alongside Briana. Is it possible she's actually being nice? No, there has to be another explanation.

When the bell rings, I jump to my feet and race out into the hallway.

"Did you see that?" I whisper as Marisol catches up to me. "Caitlin just sat there."

Marisol nods. "That was pretty weird. Though Caitlin hasn't really been acting like herself lately."

"She hasn't?"

"Haven't you noticed how quiet she's been the past few weeks?"

I haven't noticed, but of course I've had my own issues to worry about. Caitlin's always been quieter and less obnoxious than Briana, but is there more to it than that?

After we take our seats in math class, Marisol leans over my desk, grinning. "So…tell me more about Evan Riley."

My cheeks instantly flare up.

"Ha!" she says, like she's caught me red-handed. "I knew you thought he was cute! Does this mean Stephanie is finally out of the picture?" *Stephanie* is our code name for Steve Mueller, so we can talk about him at school without worrying about anyone overhearing. When I don't say anything back, Marisol groans and smacks me with her Algebra homework. "Rachel, you know he's dating Briana! Not to mention the fact that his friends have been making your life a living hell all year."

"Stephanie's not like the rest of them," I insist. "He's never said a word to me about the Troy thing." Granted, Steve has barely said a word to me about anything. "I know he's a nice guy. Remember that time last year when—"

"When he was your knight in shining armor?" Marisol rolls her eyes. "The guy does one nice thing, and you think he's a saint."

One day last spring, I was so busy gawking at Steve in the cafeteria that I somehow dropped my lunch money in the trash by accident. Steve saw what happened, and he stood there in front of the whole cafeteria and fished around in the mess of apple cores and ketchup-stained napkins until he found the money. I don't care what Marisol says. Steve Mueller is amazing.

"He didn't have to help me, but he totally did!" I insist.

Marisol shakes her head. "All I know is, your perfect guy shouldn't be dating your arch nemesis."

She has a point. And there's no way Steve will notice me when he has a girlfriend like Briana. But those hours of sniffing bleach over the weekend must have melted my brain because I can't help thinking there's a chance that one day, somehow, Steve Mueller could be mine.

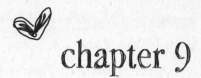

chapter 9

The next day at school, I spend all morning stressing about how little money I've managed to save up. I have just over three weeks before Mom looks at the account balance, and the only increase in my peanut-butter-jar savings is thanks to forty-seven cents I found in a pair of jeans.

I wish I could get another job, but when I asked Mom about it last night, she went on a tirade about how I need to focus on school. I couldn't exactly tell her why the money is so important, so I had to drop the whole thing. I'm starting to understand how Mom feels worrying about cash all the time. I've already told Marisol that if I start putting labels on random things, she has my permission to shake me.

I'm so busy trying to figure out how to earn some more money that I'm not paying attention as I make my way to lunch. I swing around the corner and slam right into Mr. Hammond, the vice principal.

"Oof!" he says as my shoulder jabs into his round stomach.

I jump back and drop my bag on the floor. Notebooks and pencils spill out on the linoleum, along with my cooking journal.

"Rachel Lee!" Mr. Hammond says, rubbing his belly as I scramble to pick up my things. "That's quite the tackle you've got there. You should try out for the football team next year."

I have no idea how he knows who I am. I've never been in trouble or anything. Most of my teachers have a hard time remembering my name, and it's almost the end of the year.

"I–I'm sorry," I say, straightening up. I go to take a step backward, and my foot slides on something. I skid along the floor and land on my back. For some reason, my torso suddenly feels cold.

I look down and—OH MY GOLDFISH! My shirt is up by my shoulders and my sports bra, the ratty one I've had since sixth grade, is on display for everyone. Including Mr. Hammond!

I shriek and try to sit up so I can pull my shirt back down, but I only manage to slam my head into something. When I hear a loud grunt, I realize my head crashed right into Mr. Hammond's chin.

"I'm sorry!" I cry, finally managing to yank my shirt back into place.

I hear people laughing all around us. Mr. Hammond tries to help me up, but I push him away as I scramble to my feet. I spot a pencil on the floor. That must be what tripped me. Stupid, evil pencil.

"Are you all right?" Mr. Hammond says.

I barely hear him because at that moment an all-too-familiar laugh echoes through the hallway, louder than all the others.

Briana Riley is leaning against her locker, watching the whole scene. There's a look on her face like she just won the jackpot. "Nice bra," she mouths before striding off and disappearing around the corner.

Out of nowhere, a tear drips down my cheek and onto one of my muddy shoes.

"Rachel?" Mr. Hammond says, his voice loud and alarmed now. "I said, are you all right? Do you need to go to the nurse?"

I shake my head, wiping my face with my sleeve. I can't believe I'm crying in the middle of the hallway! "I'm fine," I manage to say before I grab my bag and dart away.

Instead of going to the cafeteria, I head toward the only place that can make me feel better: the Home Ec room.

Ms. Kennedy is hanging up charts for the sixth-grade nutrition unit when I come in. As usual, she has flour on the front of her shirt and a wooden spoon stuck through her messy bun. Her face lights up when she spots me.

"Rachel Lee!" she says. "Haven't seen you in a while." She grabs an apron from a nearby hook and holds it out to me. "Come to blow off some steam?"

I nod as I gratefully take the apron and then pull it over my head.

"Are you all right?" she asks, peering into my face.

I nod again, not trusting myself to say anything. Crying once today is more than enough.

"Okay," Ms. Kennedy says. "Well, you know the drill. Feel free to use whatever you find in the fridge." She gives me another long look before going back to her charts.

Even though my entire body is shaking, I ignore it and get to work, grabbing eggs and cocoa powder and anything else that feels right. I don't exactly have a plan, but I know I have to make something that will stop the tears still stinging at my eyes. Sea salt brownies, I finally decide.

As I start whisking flour, baking powder, and salt together, I can feel my breathing slow down, and the jittery feeling in my entire body starts to fade. My mortifying fall and Briana's horrible laugh keep replaying in my head until the smells of chocolate and butter and vanilla start to take over. Soon, all I'm thinking about is the recipe. Melt chocolate in double-boiler. Mix wet ingredients. Fold in dry ingredients. Pour into pan.

Finally, everything is ready to go in the oven. When the timer is set for twenty-five minutes, I turn to see Ms. Kennedy smiling at me from across the room.

"Feeling better?" she asks.

"Yeah," I say, realizing it's true. Maybe I'm still not a happy bunny, but I can breathe again. I go over and help Ms. Kennedy staple nutrition handouts and cut up carrot sticks for students to snack on during class. We don't say much as we work, but Ms. Kennedy is one of those rare people who don't seem to mind silence. Sometimes I wonder if food is a language all in itself.

When the bell rings, marking the end of lunch, Ms. Kennedy just smiles and writes out a pass for me so I can stay until my brownies are done. Why can't all my teachers be this understanding?

After the timer goes off, I sprinkle some chocolate chips on top of the brownies. When they melt a bit, I spread them around evenly and then put some coarse sea salt on top, tapping the pan to make the crystals set into the chocolate. Once the brownies cool down a little, I fork a piece into my mouth.

"Mmm," I say as the chocolate melts on my tongue. The saltiness perfectly matches my mood.

"Wow," says Ms. Kennedy as she tries a bite. "These sure are bold. I don't know if I'd use quite so much salt next time."

I swallow another bite, realizing she's right. The brownies might be exactly what I needed today, but they're probably too intense for the bake sale.

After I'm done taking pictures of the brownies and making notes in my journal, I pull off my apron. "Thanks, Ms. Kennedy," I say before heading for the door.

"Don't you want to take the rest of your brownies?"

"That's okay. You can give them to your class if you want."

"I don't know if that will send the right message about nutrition, but I'm sure the students won't object." She laughs and gives me a little wave. "Come back anytime."

I wave back and head out the door, ready to face things again.

Though the one thing I'm absolutely *not* ready for is the sight of Steve Mueller—*the* Steve Mueller—leaning against my locker.

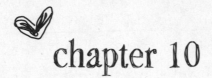

chapter 10

When Steve Mueller sees me coming toward him, he stands up straight and runs his hand through his spiky hair. Steve Mueller is looking at me! Steve Mueller is smiling at me!

"You're Rachel, right?"

Steve Mueller is talking to me! I nod and bite my bottom lip to keep down a hysterical giggle.

"Listen, I wanted to ask you something." He waves me over as if he has a secret to tell me. I float toward him, my feet numb, as if my brain needs extra blood to process what's happening. "So," he says in a low voice, "Briana was telling me you've been cleaning her house."

Oh, holy eggplant. Is Marisol right? Is Steve really just a jerk, and he's here to make fun of me too? What if he heard about my hallway wipeout?

His eyebrows go up. "Is that right?"

I nod again, my head moving in slow motion. Why does my whole body seem to slow down whenever there's a cute guy around?

"So listen," Steve goes on. "I was wondering if you could do me a favor. See, Briana's been acting kind of weird lately. I'm not saying she's cheating on me or anything, but…" He shrugs his perfect shoulders. "Anyway, I thought maybe you could keep an eye out when you're at her place and let me know if you find anything."

I blink back at him. The thought of anyone cheating on Steve Mueller is insane. He's the hottest guy in school! Those sparkling eyes. That strong chin. And those dimples!

"Well, what do you think?" he says.

Wait. Is he really asking me to spy on Briana? If he thinks she might be cheating on him, shouldn't he just talk to her?

"Hello? Anyone in there?" Steve laughs, but I can tell he's getting impatient.

"Um. Er," I articulately reply. "Maybe?"

"Okay, you're right." He holds his hands up in defeat and takes a step closer, his blue-smelling cologne washing over me. "You're wondering what's in it for you." He pulls a twenty-dollar bill out of his pocket. "How about I give you this now, and when you have some info for me, I'll give you twenty more. Deal?"

I stare at the bill like it's made out of gold. It took me all day to earn that much on Saturday, and here Steve Mueller is giving it to me for nothing. Okay, for spying. But if Briana really is cheating on him, then doesn't he have a right to know?

"Well?"

"Um." I know I shouldn't agree to this. It's wrong. Even though Briana is evil. Even though Mom will murder me if she finds out I spent some of my college money. I'm not the kind of girl who spies on people.

But when I open my mouth to say so, a long squeaking sound comes out instead.

"All right!" says Steve. "Thanks for helping me out." He slips the bill into my hand, and I almost faint at the feel of his warm skin on mine. Then he flashes a bright smile, dimples and all. "I'll see you around."

My heart melts and starts oozing down the insides of my chest like chocolate sauce. Wait, did I just agree to spy on Briana Riley? And, more importantly, does that mean there's a chance Steve Mueller might actually talk to me again?

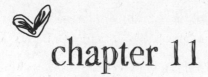

chapter 11

That night I spend almost an hour rearranging my bookshelves to get them back to normal. Mom snuck into my bedroom while I was watching a cooking show and put all my books in alphabetical order. If Dad doesn't come home soon, I'm afraid she'll start trying to alphabetize my clothes next.

As I finish putting the last of my cookbooks on one shelf, my cell phone rings.

"Hi there, Rachel Roo."

"Hi, Dad. How's Florida?" I try to keep the bitterness out of my voice. If I let on how upset I am about him leaving, it might scare him off and then he'll never come home.

"Oh, you know," he says, chuckling. "I've got sand everywhere, even in my ears. But otherwise good."

"How's the scuba business going?" I ask. What I'm really asking is: Have you finally given up on your crazy-face dream?

"There's been a little more red tape than I expected with permits and things, but it should all be sorted out soon. Tell your mom I'll be sending her some money any day now."

"I'll tell her." Of course I won't, because he made the exact same promise last month, and we never got any money.

"What's new with you, Roo?"

I want to tell him about Mom's latest weird behavior, but when I mentioned her labeling obsession to him last week, he just laughed it off like it wasn't a big deal. I hope he's right.

Since I don't even want to think about everything that's been happening at school, I start telling him about all the brownie recipes I've been trying out for the bake sale. "I was thinking of perfecting cheesecake brownies next, since they're your favorite."

"What does your mom think about you spending so much time baking?"

So much for luring Dad back home with baked goods. "She keeps saying that if my grades start slipping, I'm cut off. But I don't know if she'd really do that. Her boss has been way nicer to her ever since she started bringing leftover brownies in to work."

Dad laughs. "Even stuffy lawyers love chocolate." He

starts doing an over-the-top impression of Mom's boss, which makes me laugh too. But laughing with Dad only makes me miss him more.

"Don't you want to come home?" I can't help asking, my voice wobbling.

"Roo, of course I do. But this was just something I had to try out. When you come to visit this summer, you'll see just how great it is down here."

My heart starts hammering away. I just have to act normal so he doesn't suspect anything. To make my Get-Parents-Back-Together Plan work, I had to tell Dad that Mom knows all about the trip. Since she still refuses to talk to him after what he did to us, I can get away with lying. At least for now. Normally I'd feel horrible about being so sneaky, but I don't really have a choice.

"While we're on the topic, I have a special surprise for you," Dad goes on. "I was going to wait until you came down here, but I just can't keep it a secret any longer. How would you like to go see a taping of your favorite show?"

I blink. "Do you mean *Pastry Wars*?"

"That's right. It turns out they're shooting an episode right near here in July. So I was thinking that I could buy some tickets and we could go see the taping together."

"Holy avocado dip, are you serious? That would be amazing!"

"I'll have to clear it with your mom, of course. But I don't see why she should object."

"*No!*" I yell, almost dropping the phone. "Er, I mean, don't say anything to her yet. She's been on this real money-saving kick, and she might not approve of us going to see the show." My lungs feel like they're burning. I hate lying, but there's no other choice.

"It's my money I'll be spending," he says. "She should be all right with it."

I want to ask Dad how he has money to spend on the tickets and none to send to us, but I don't want to start an argument. Besides, how can I pass up a chance to see my favorite show? "Dad, she still doesn't want to talk to you. Just give her some more time." At least that part's mostly true.

"I guess you're right." He sighs. "I can't wait for you to come down here, Rachel. We'll have a great time, just the two of us, okay?"

I close my eyes. It sounds perfect. "Okay," I tell him. "I'll be there."

chapter 12

The next morning I go to grab my journal and almost shriek when I see tons of little neon tabs sticking out of it. I flip it open, and sure enough, Mom went through and labeled all my recipes. As if that's not bad enough, she tried to put the recipes into categories, ones that are completely wrong. And she used the permanent kinds of tabs that'll rip the pages if I try to take them off. It's like someone taking a Bible and drawing on it with glitter paint.

When I flip to the "Dirt Diary" part, I almost shriek all over again as I remember what I wrote about how cute Evan Riley is. I expect there to be a tab with "Rachel's Crush" scribbled on it, but I guess I'm in luck because the pages are untouched. Thank goodness I wrote down my notes in the very back of the notebook where Mom wouldn't think to look.

"Mom!" I yell. "Mom, come here!"

She comes running, clearly thinking there's a fire or something. "What is it? What's wrong?"

"How could you do this?" I say, holding up the journal. I'm so mad that my hands are shaking.

She looks at me like I'm the crazy one. "What do you mean? I just organized it for you. It should make things easier now."

"Easier? You messed it up! You had no right to take my personal property!"

"Oh really, Rachel. You're being so melodramatic about this. It's just some recipes."

"Not just some recipes, Mom. *My* recipes. My *life* is in here!"

She rolls her eyes. "Fine, that's the last time I do you a favor. Now finish getting ready and come eat breakfast."

As I hear her go down the hall, my whole face is throbbing like it might explode. I suck in a few breaths, trying to calm down. I wish more than anything that Dad were here. He'd wrap me up in a hug and tell me he'd find a way to make things better. Then again, if Dad hadn't left, Mom would never have attacked my journal in the first place.

I let out a sputtering sigh and carefully put my journal

down like it's a burn victim, hoping Marisol might be able to figure out a way to fix it. When I stomp into the kitchen to grab some cereal, Mom's sipping coffee and looking at house listings online.

"Before I forget, we have a couple new cleaning jobs," she says, all calm and normal as if nothing happened. "So have your homework done and be ready to go when I get home from work tonight."

"Tonight? I thought we were just going to do weekends."

"We were, but I can't say no to new clients. You don't have anything else going on Thursday nights, right?"

That's not exactly true. They always replay episodes of *Pastry Wars* on Thursdays, and I like to study the episodes to see what wisdom I can get out of them. But that doesn't mean anything to Mom except time away from my schoolwork. Anyway, more houses equal more money.

"Whose places are we doing?" I ask, expecting her to list more names of kids I know.

And sure enough, she says: "The Singhs'. Their sons go to your school. They're twins."

I nod. The Singh twins are a year younger than me, but since they're the only pair of completely identical twins in the entire school, everyone knows who they are. Luckily,

I'm almost positive they have no idea who I am, so hopefully I can get in and out of there unscathed.

"And also Robert Hammond's house," Mom adds.

I almost spit out a bite of cereal. "Robert Hammond as in my vice principal?"

"It's funny how things work out," Mom says, sitting down beside me at the table. "He called me to talk about you last night, and somehow we got on the topic of cleaning."

Oh, holy mango sorbet. "Mr. Hammond called you about me? What did he say?" I can just imagine him telling Mom all about my wardrobe malfunction and emotional meltdown in the hallway.

She laughs at what must be total terror on my face. "Don't look so worried, Rachel. I guess he heard our family was going through a rough patch, and he wanted to see if there was anything he could do to help."

"And now we're going to clean his house?"

"His wife passed away a few years ago, and he doesn't have any children. I think it'll cheer him up to have us take care of things."

After everything that happened in school the other day, how can I face Mr. Hammond? I was hoping to get through the rest of the year without crossing paths with him again, and now I'm supposed to go mop his floors? I just have to keep thinking about the money, I tell myself. And hope the humiliation doesn't kill me.

chapter 13

Mr. Hammond's house is nothing like I expected. I thought everything would be beige and blah, but it's actually kind of amazing. He has sports memorabilia everywhere, including more Red Sox stuff than I've ever seen in one place. And even though his kitchen isn't as gleaming as Briana Riley's, it's huge and stocked with every gadget and utensil you can imagine.

"I love to cook," he says. "And, if you can't tell, I love to eat." He jokingly grabs his belly, which makes my cheeks flush as I remember how I slammed into him in the hallway. He hasn't mentioned anything about that whole mess. I'm hoping it was so traumatic that he permanently blocked it out.

"Don't be silly, Robert," Mom says. "You look great. Most men your age would kill to be as fit as you are."

Mr. Hammond grins, while I stare. Since when is Mom so chummy with my vice principal?

"Where should we start?" she asks.

"Wherever you like, Amanda." His grin widens until it's in Cheshire Cat territory. "I know you always have a plan."

Mom giggles, actually *giggles*. "Oh, Robert," she says. Then she glances at me, like she just remembered I'm in the room. "You probably don't know this, but Mr. Hammond and I went to school together."

Seriously? I thought Mr. Hammond was about a million years old. But as I look at him again, I notice he actually has less gray hair than my dad.

"Your mom was one smart cookie back then," he says. "Still is."

Mom giggles again and tucks her hair behind her ears. Why is she acting so weird? Wait. Is it possible she's actually *flirting* with Mr. Hammond?

"All right, we don't want to take up your whole evening," she says, still smiling. "I guess we can start in the kitchen."

"No need to hurry," he says. "My evenings are pretty boring. Mostly catching up on work and trying out new recipes."

My ears perk up. "Recipes? What kind?"

Mr. Hammond shrugs. "Anything, really. I used to want to be a chef when I was younger. But I never quite had the talent for it."

"Wow, really?" I've never met anyone besides Ms. Kennedy who's as much into food as I am.

"Your mom tells me you like to cook too. Have you taken any classes?" Mr. Hammond asks.

"I want to. There are a few at the community college, but they're pretty expensive." I'm about to tell him about a candy-making class I'd like to sign up for, but Mom calls me over to help her clean the counters.

"Don't want to keep your mom waiting," says Mr. Hammond. "I know how impatient she can be."

"No kidding!" I hurry over to the kitchen while he goes into the living room and turns on the TV. I can't believe I just had something like a friendly conversation with the vice principal and survived!

"Do you mind doing the bathroom?" Mom asks.

I grab some supplies and head down the hall. The bathroom looks pretty spotless, but I start spraying every surface anyway.

When I'm done cleaning, I notice the cabinet under the sink won't close all the way. I open it and find a sponge blocking the door. After I move it aside and go to shut the cabinet, I spot something that nearly makes me shriek.

Adult diapers. Tons of them. At least three packs. Oh my goldfish, Mr. Hammond wears diapers!

"Rachel, are you done in there?" Mom calls.

I slam the cabinet shut, trying to swallow down the laughter bubbling inside me, and hurry out into the hallway. As I pass by the living room, I try not to look in Mr. Hammond's direction or I'll totally lose it. *Diapers*!

"Do you need help finding anything?" he asks me.

I shake my head, biting my lip so hard I can almost taste blood, and quickly get to work dusting a nearby bookcase. I can hear Mom whistling from down the hallway, like she's never been happier.

"Rachel," says Mr. Hammond, turning down the volume on the TV. "I just wanted to say that I was really sorry to hear about your father leaving. I know how hard that can be."

The laughter I've been holding in disappears. I keep dusting the same shelf over and over, not sure what to say.

Mr. Hammond clears his throat. "I guess what I'm getting at is that I know your mom's tough, that she can handle it. And I know you're tough too. You two will be just fine."

I can't believe it. He's talking like it's over, like my dad deserted us and there's no chance he'll ever come back.

"We're already fine," I blurt out. "My dad's just away on business. He's coming back."

Mr. Hammond blinks in confusion. "I thought...your mother said...I'm sorry. I must have misunderstood."

"You did." I grab the dusting spray and storm away. "Mom, I'll be in the car," I call. I don't even wait for an answer before I turn and get the Helsinki out of there.

chapter 14

After we're done with our cleaning jobs for the night, I convince Mom to drop me off at Marisol's house so I can have her fix my journal. I expect Mom to yell at me for rushing out of Mr. Hammond's house like that, but she seems to be in her own little world. She has the radio turned up louder than usual, and she keeps humming along to every cheesy song that comes on. I pray it has nothing to do with the giggling (and possible flirting) I witnessed earlier.

When we get to Marisol's house, Mom reaches into her pocket and pulls out ten dollars. "Here, for your hard work tonight."

"Wow, thanks."

Mom looks like she's about to say more, but then she just nods and gives me a stiff smile. I wonder if the money is her way of apologizing for what she did to my journal.

Or maybe it's out of guilt for going all gaga over another man right in front of me. After all, getting paid twenty bucks for an entire day of labor and ten for a couple hours' worth doesn't really add up.

"Have fun with Marisol," she says as I get out of the car. Then she starts singing along to another cheesy song as I close the door behind me.

I'm glad to get away from Mom's weird behavior, but I'm also nervous about seeing Marisol. I've been trying to figure out the best way to tell her about my conversation with Steve Mueller without her freaking out about it.

As I go up the front walkway, I spot Angela Bareli sitting on the porch next door, like she always seems to be doing whenever I go over to visit Marisol. My theory is that she stays out there so she can spy on everyone in the neighborhood and gather gossip.

Angela isn't usually too bad when she isn't trying to impress Briana, but I still try to avoid eye contact with her as I hurry to ring Marisol's doorbell. Unfortunately, Angela calls out my name, leaving me no choice but to stop and talk to her.

"Are you doing the bake sale again this year?" she asks.

"Yup. Are you?"

Angela smiles. "Absolutely. Do you know what you're making this time? Last year was what, pecan pie?"

"Caramel pecan squares." The best I've ever made. I got tons of votes too, but Angela still beat me with her chocolate peanut-butter cookies. I might not love being the center of attention, but I know my food can outshine Angela's. And that hundred-dollar prize will bring me one huge step closer to getting my family back together. "Not sure what I'm making this year."

"Well, good luck," Angela says with a too-bright smile.

"Thanks," I mumble before rushing away to the safety of Marisol's house.

"I'm so glad you're here," Marisol says when she opens the door. "I need your opinion on something." She waves for me to follow her upstairs.

Marisol's house isn't as flashy as most of the other houses in the neighborhood, but it's still pretty fancy. It feels cozy, though, like it's meant to be lived in instead of displayed. The couches are plush and inviting, and Marisol's cat, Chanel, is always nearby waiting for a scratch behind the ears. The walls are painted in bold reds and oranges, and Marisol's bright handmade quilts hang all over the house. Even though two of Marisol's brothers are away at college and the third one is almost never home, I can still feel the energy of all those people in the house, so different from my almost-empty one.

When we get to Marisol's bedroom, I gasp. The most beautiful dress I've ever seen is spread out on the bed. It's red and sparkly and looks like something a movie star would wear.

"Do you like it?" she asks. "I still have to sew on some more sequins, but I think it came out pretty good."

"It's gorgeous!" I run my fingers over the cool satin. It's easily the prettiest thing she's ever made.

"I'll have to take some pictures once it's done and put them online." Marisol has a website where she posts photos of all her creations. Hardly anyone visits it, but hopefully one day a famous person will see it and want Marisol to make clothes for them. "Now I have to figure out where to wear it," she adds with a shrug. "I guess I could just wear it to school."

"No! You can't waste something like that on a regular school day. It has to be for a special occasion."

Marisol smiles. "I do have a math test coming up next week."

"You know what I mean."

She picks up the dress, and the entire thing shimmers

in the light like a disco ball. I can't stop looking at it until Marisol finally puts it in her closet and shuts the door.

"So what's new?" she asks, coming to sit on the bed.

I know it's time to tell Marisol about Steve Mueller. The secret is sitting in my chest like heartburn. But when I open my mouth to tell her, I realize I'm crazy to think I can come clean. If I admit to Marisol that I'm considering spying on Briana, she'll be so disappointed in me. I'll tell her later, I decide, after I figure out what to do and it's too late for her to try to change my mind.

"I need your help," I say instead, carefully taking my journal out of my bag. I explain what happened and show Marisol the neon tabs.

"Let me see that." The determined tone in her voice makes me relax. If anyone can put my journal back the way it was, it's Marisol. She grabs some scissors and other crafty supplies and gets to work. "What's this?" she asks after a minute.

Oh no. She's found the Dirt Diary. In all the craziness, I forgot to tear out the pages before giving it to her.

"Just some notes to myself," I say. "About our cleaning jobs the other day."

Marisol's eyebrows keep going up as she scans the pages. "What do you plan on doing with these notes?"

"Nothing. They're just for me. No one else is supposed to read them." I think of my mom and how close she was to discovering the diary. "Anyway, I'll be careful."

That seems to be enough for Marisol because she gets back to fixing the journal. "So what else has been going on?" she asks.

I tell her about cleaning the Singhs' house. Both twins were out of the house, so the only sign of them was the dirty laundry all over their room. And yes, I had to pull on gloves and put their smelly boxers into the hamper before I could vacuum. I will never look at the twins again without shuddering.

"Then we cleaned Mr. Hammond's house," I say, grabbing a handmade pig-shaped pillow and hugging it tight.

"Was that weird after the whole hallway incident?" she asks, flashing me a sympathetic look. Even Marisol, who's practically incapable of being embarrassed, still cringed when I told her about my moment of bra-flashing glory.

"Not as bad as I was expecting," I say. "It turns out he went to school with my mom."

"Really? I wonder what she was like back then."

"According to Mr. Hammond, pretty much the same. He was going on about how smart she was." I know my mom's big regret in life is not going to college. She took time off after high school to work and save up for tuition, but then she met my dad and had me and college went out the window. She claims having me was a great trade-off, but I can't help wondering sometimes. That's probably why she's always telling me I have to focus on my future. "She was acting pretty weird when we first got there, though, all giggly and stuff."

"Maybe she was flirting with him," Marisol says, carefully snipping off one of the tabs.

"No way!" I say, a little too loudly. If even Marisol thinks Mom might have been flirting, then maybe it really is true.

"Well, your mom is single now, right?"

I almost choke. "What? She's not single. She's married."

"I know that. I just mean—"

"Even if my mom was interested in other men, which she isn't, she'd never be into Mr. Hammond. He's the vice principal!"

"So?" says Marisol.

"And he wears diapers!"

Marisol puts down her scissors and looks at me like I've just turned into an elephant. "What are you talking about?"

"Don't repeat this to anyone, okay?" When she promises not to, I tell her about my discovery in the bathroom. "See, there's no way my mom would be into him. And anyway, she isn't interested in anyone besides my dad, so don't even say that, okay?"

Marisol raises her hands in surrender. "Sorry. I didn't mean anything by it. I was just saying that if your parents do stay split up, eventually your mom might—"

"That won't happen! I'm doing all of this so I can get them back together, remember?"

"Okay, I get it. I'm sorry," says Marisol. I can tell by the look on her face that she means it, but I also realize that Marisol doesn't really understand. I wonder if there's anyone who really does.

chapter 15

In the morning I make sure to pack my journal in my school bag so Mom can't get her hands on it again.

Marisol worked her magic and managed to get most of the tabs off the pages without ripping them. The ones that did rip, she carefully patched together. I almost cried when she gave the notebook back to me all in one piece. When I got home, I promptly updated the Dirt Diary with details about the houses we cleaned last night. I described Mr. Hammond's house and his diapers, but omitted my mom's flirting and what he'd said about my dad. Those weren't things I wanted to put in writing. I also made sure not to mention anything about Steve Mueller's offer.

I find Mom paying bills online at the kitchen table. I have to keep my heart from thumping out of my chest as I make some breakfast. Since she's not trying to choke me to death, that must mean she hasn't looked at my college-fund balance yet. If all goes well, I still have about three weeks left before I have to grow a mustache, change my name, and leave the country.

When I sit down beside her, Mom lets out a long sigh and murmurs, "I hope we get a check from your father soon. It would really help with expenses."

I'm surprised to hear her bring up Dad. She's barely wanted to talk about him since he left.

"Do you miss him?" I can't help asking.

"Of course," she says softly, her eyes getting squinty. "But your father expected us to uproot our entire lives for one of his whims. We have family and friends and responsibilities here, and he wanted us to just drop all of that." Her voice gets louder, and her cheeks start turning pink. "He made the decision by himself, and he can deal with the consequences when it crashes and burns."

"But would you forgive him if he came back?" *Please, please, please?*

"Oh, Rachel. I know you miss your father, but I can't just take him back unless he's willing to grow up."

I've heard Mom say that for years, that Dad has to stop acting like a child. My parents never really argued, but sometimes Dad would do something impulsive and drive Mom nuts. Like the time he got me a kitten for my tenth birthday without running it by her first. We had to give it away since Dad didn't remember that Mom was allergic. He apologized and tickled Mom until she laughed and forgave him. I don't think that approach will work this time.

"But what if—?"

"Please, Rachel. Enough," she says, rubbing her temples like our conversation is making her head ache. "And don't bother asking if you can go visit him again. I told you, your father can't be counted on."

Any hopes of Mom changing her mind seep out of me. How on earth am I going to convince her to let me go to Florida once she finds out I've bought a ticket? I take a deep breath and tell myself that I'll figure it out when the time comes. I have to.

"I know it's hard," Mom goes on, "but sometimes we just have to move on. That's what life is all about."

I don't think life is about bulldozing your way through situations and not even attempting to make things work, but I don't want to argue anymore. Mom is mad enough already. If I do manage to get Dad to come home, I want there to be a possibility that she'll put all that anger aside and actually give him a chance. Otherwise, all the lies I've been telling will be for nothing.

chapter 16

I spend all day Friday avoiding Mr. Hammond, which isn't easy. How did I not notice before that he's all over the school? Every time I see him, all I can think about (besides adult diapers) is what Marisol said. Is it possible my mom really will start dating again? I try to purge the idea from my head, but it stays stuck there like a piece of old gum.

At least everyone else leaves me alone. Caitlin is still being strangely quiet, and Briana's in full-on concentration mode for the big softball game this afternoon, so she's ignoring everyone around her. I used to think everyone has some kind of redeeming quality, but with Briana I'm not sure her talent at softball is all that redeeming. It just lets her chuck balls at people.

My only close call is the sight of one of the Singh twins walking down the hall after lunch. My skin immediately starts itching, like I'm holding his dirty underwear all over again. I dart into the bathroom and splash cold water on my face until the itchy feeling fades. Who knew cleaning people's bedrooms could be so traumatizing?

I'm relieved when the last bell rings and it's finally time to go home. That is, until I can't get my locker open. After a bunch of useless tugging and pounding, I have to ask the janitor for help.

It takes him a few tries with a variety of tools, but finally he manages to saw his way in.

"Looks like it was glued shut," he says. "Someone must have played a joke on you."

It doesn't take a genius to figure out who that was, especially when I find a note in my locker that says: "I'm stuck on you, Rachel. Love, Troy." My books aren't ruined, but my fleece is caked with dried glue. And I have to slam my locker three times before it clicks shut. Plus, when I rush out of the building to try to catch my bus, it's long gone. I'll have to walk the three miles home. Perfect.

It's windy out, so I throw on my crusty fleece as I cut behind the school past the softball field. As I hurry along, I can hear people cheering for our team, and someone even calls out Briana's name. How can she be so evil and still have people rooting for her?

"Look, it's that maid girl," a seventh-grade girl says to her friend as they walk by me. They both laugh, and I hear them say something about a sports bra.

Blood pounds in my ears. I hate Briana. When I think about Steve asking me to spy on her, I realize I don't feel so bad about it anymore. If she can go out of her way to laugh at me and play pranks on me, why can't I rifle through a few of her drawers? She started the war in the first place.

As another cheer erupts from the crowd, I glance over at the softball field and spot Evan Riley standing by the bleachers. I freeze. Part of me wants to make a run for it so he won't see me. But another part of me wants to stay put since I'm actually kind of excited to see him again.

After a second, probably feeling my creepy stare, Evan turns and looks right at me. And then he smiles. I suck in my breath like I've just been hit in the stomach. I want to run. I want to stay. So I just stand there.

As he comes toward me, I realize I'm still wearing the glue-covered fleece. But it's too late to rip it off and shove it in my bag.

"Hey, Booger Crap," he says with a grin. "Are you here to watch the game?"

I shake my head. "Just going home."

"It's supposed to be a good one. The other team is the best in the district. Briana's pitching really well so far." He glances over his shoulder as the crowd lets out another cheer. "Usually I have baseball practice after school, so I don't get to see her play much. But the coach canceled today. Are you sure you don't want to stick around?"

His tone is so friendly that I'm actually tempted to stay, but I don't think I can handle the sight of Briana. "Sorry, I can't."

"Oh well. Maybe another time." He reaches into his pocket and takes out a handful of peppermint candies. "Want one?"

I shake my head. The last thing I need today is to accidentally choke to death on a piece of hard candy.

Evan shrugs as he pops one into his mouth and starts crunching away. Then he gives me a crooked grin. "I steal them from my dad's office. They're kind of addicting."

That explains Evan's yummy peppermint smell the other day. Oh my goldfish. Did I just call a guy's scent *yummy*? On cue, my cheeks start to burn.

"Well, I'll let you get going," says Evan. "But I'll see you at my house tomorrow, right?" He sounds so genuine that it makes me relax a little bit.

"I'll be there," I say.

"Great, I'll—"

"Hey, Riley!" another guy says, coming up to us. He has curly blond hair and eyes the color of Windex. (Yup, apparently I've started comparing things to cleaning products.) The guy looks me up and down. "Who's this?"

"This is Rachel," says Evan. "Rachel, this is Kurt. We play baseball together."

"Hey," Kurt says, giving me a little nod, his eyes still on me like he's trying to see through my shirt. At least I'm wearing normal undergarments today. The old sports bra has been sent off to the dresser in the sky.

His gaze makes me feel so icked out that when I try to say hello, nothing comes out but air.

"Are you mute or something?" Kurt says with a smile that looks more like a sneer. "Or do I just make you speechless?"

I don't even know how to respond to that.

"Hello?" says Kurt, so loudly that the whole crowd behind us can probably hear. "Anyone home?"

"Wow, Kurt," says Evan. "I don't blame her for not wanting to talk to you when you're being such a jerk."

"I'm just trying to be friendly. She's the one who's acting like I'm not even here." He leans in and gets right in my face. "You do see me, right? You're not blind or something? And what's that crap all over your jacket?"

His hot breath makes my eyes water. I step back, and his smirk tells me what he's thinking. That I'm a loser. That he doesn't know why someone like Evan would be talking to me. And of course, he's right.

"I have to go," I manage to whisper. Without giving either of them another look, I hurry away.

chapter 17

When I get home, I grab a brownie pan and a bowl from the cupboard and start mixing ingredients without even thinking about what I'm doing. I can't stop replaying the whole scene with Evan and Kurt in my head. I don't care what Kurt thinks, but if Evan wasn't already convinced I'm a freak, he is now. I mean, I just stood there like a statue and then ran away!

I throw down the spoon I'm holding and tear off my glue-caked fleece. Then I open the kitchen window and chuck it out into the bushes.

As I start stirring ingredients again, I think back to everything that's happened since the beginning of the school year. When I started eighth grade, some part of me hoped that things would be different, that I'd stop being so painfully shy, that people would actually notice me, maybe even like me. But instead, everything has just gotten worse.

I go to the spice cabinet and grab the first bottle I see: cayenne pepper. Perfect. I dump some into the batter and keep stirring. The biting smell goes up my nose, and somehow the combination of that and the chocolate finally starts to calm me down.

By the time the oven finishes preheating, I'm feeling better. But I still jump when Mom opens the front door.

"Ray-chul?" She does *not* sound happy. When she comes into the kitchen, I can see why. She's holding my glue-covered—and now muddy—fleece in her hand. "What was this doing outside?"

"Um." How can I explain without her storming into Mr. Hammond's office on Monday morning and demanding that Briana be punished? Things are bad enough without Briana telling everyone I'm a snitch. "I spilled glue on it," I finally say.

"And then you just decided to toss it into the azaleas?"

"Maybe?"

"Are you really this thoughtless? Can't you see we don't have the money to just be throwing things away?"

"I know. I'm sorry."

I expect her to start furiously scrubbing at the fleece, trying to clean it to death, but instead she drapes it over one of the kitchen chairs and sinks down into another one. Her shoulders are rounded, like she's too tired to sit up straight. "I thought we were a team, Rachel."

"We are," I say, though the words feel fake and hollow coming out of my mouth.

She looks over, and her eyes seem to bore right into me. I expect her to call me out on everything: taking the money, lying to Dad, and lying to her. But instead, she gives me a sad smile and says, "We only have each other now. That means we have to work together, okay?"

I want to yell that it's not just us, that Dad will be coming back any day now. But then I remember that I have to act like the dutiful daughter who can't wait to go clean another house, because if Mom starts to suspect anything, then my plan will be over.

"I know, Mom," I force myself to say. "We're a team."

Some of the wrinkles on her forehead fade. "Do you want to help me work on the basement tonight?" she asks, which I know is her attempt at being nice. She already did two rounds of cleaning in the basement, so I can't imagine what kind of super-crazy organizing she has in mind.

"Um, I can't. I have to—" The oven timer goes off, saving me from having to make up an excuse.

"Are you making some kind of spicy chocolate?" Mom asks. "It smells delicious."

I nod, surprised to hear her say something about my cooking other than what a waste of time it is. I dish out a couple of portions, too impatient to wait until the brownies cool down. When I take a bite, the cayenne burns in my belly, just like my leftover anger. But when my mom's eyes start watering and I have to run and get her some water, I realize this recipe is probably too intense for the bake sale too.

At least there's one thing that came out of this awful day. My mind is finally made up: I'm going to take Steve Mueller up on his offer and spy on Briana. In fact, I can't wait to dig up her dirty secrets.

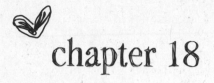

chapter 18

Saturday morning, only the dollar signs swimming around in my head get me out of bed. A little more than two weeks left and around $250 to go. It seems impossible, but I refuse to give up.

Mom is humming like a cheerful bumblebee as we pull out of the driveway. "We have a new client today." She glances over at me. "Now don't be upset, but the son is in your grade."

Here we go again. If it's Steve Mueller, I'm going to jump out of the car right now.

"His name is Andrew Ivanoff," says Mom. "Do you know him?"

I breathe a long sigh of relief. Andrew Ivanoff has the reputation of being the shyest guy in the eighth grade. We should be able to just mutely acknowledge each other and have that be the end of it.

"Yeah," I say. "I've never talked to him, but he seems okay."

Mom nods, looking relieved too. I guess she really does feel bad about inflicting people from school on me. "Normally we'll go there in the afternoons," she says, "but it'll be our first stop this morning."

The Ivanoff residence is just down the street from Marisol's house and looks almost identical except for the color. As soon as Mom and I go inside, I can see where Andrew gets his extreme shyness. Mr. Ivanoff seems nice, but he talks so quietly that I can barely hear him, and he looks over our heads like he's having a conversation with someone behind us.

Once he's shown us around the first floor of the house, he sends me up to Andrew's bedroom for a "special assignment." I pray it doesn't involve smelly underwear.

When I get to Andrew's door, I gasp.

Practically every inch of his room except for his bed is lined with toys: action figures, figurines of famous people, and a million other tiny creatures. As I get closer, I realize that's not even the weird part. Each toy is either splattered with red paint or disfigured somehow. And Andrew Ivanoff is sitting in the middle of this creepy doll parade with a cloth, gently wiping the dust off each one.

"Um, hi," I say.

Andrew's eyes shoot up, and he gawks at me like he's never seen a girl standing in his doorway before. Honestly, he probably hasn't.

"Oh," he says. "Rachel Lee." His eyes dart back toward the floor, like he's afraid I might try to hypnotize him if he looks at me for more than a second. His face and hair are so pale that I almost expect him to have red albino eyes, but they're actually the color of dark honey.

"Your dad said you needed some help?"

He nods and holds out another cloth. "The ones on this side are done," he mumbles, motioning with his head.

I carefully step in between the toys and find a clear spot on the floor by the bed. As I sit down, I accidentally knock over two My Little Ponies with missing heads. Andrew lets out a hiss like he's just been stabbed.

"Sorry," I whisper. And then I start to wipe and wipe and wipe. Most of the toys don't even have a speck of dust on them, but that doesn't seem to matter. Andrew lovingly cleans each one like it's priceless.

Finally, I can't stand it anymore. "So what are all these for?" I ask.

Andrew doesn't answer for a minute. Then he sighs and says, "For a movie."

"What movie?"

"*After the Zombie Toys Attack.*"

I bark out a laugh before I can stop myself, and Andrew's ears turn bright pink.

"Sorry," I say, trying to swallow my laughter. "It sounds…interesting."

"I start filming this week. That's why these have to be clean." He points at a tiny set on top of his desk that I didn't notice before. It's a perfect miniature replica of our school.

"That's amazing," I say. "So who'll play the students?"

"Students?" Andrew asks, oh-so-briefly glancing at me.

"Well, I'm assuming these are the zombies." I hold up an armless Dora the Explorer. "If the movie takes place at school, what are you going to use for students?"

"Everyone's dead before the movie starts," he explains in a slow, patient voice. "The story's about the zombie toys forming a community within the school."

"Do zombies have communities?" I'm not exactly a horror fan, but I've seen enough previews to know the whole point of zombie flicks is to give movie stars something to run away from.

Andrew's shoulders droop. "I don't know," he admits.

"I've been having trouble with the script. But I want to send the finished product in with my application for film camp, so I have to start shooting soon."

Film camp sounds so glamorous. Though that is definitely *not* the word I'd use to describe Andrew.

At that moment, the doorbell rings, and Andrew jumps to his feet and runs to the window. After he glances outside, his shoulders relax and he comes to sit back down.

"Are you okay?" I ask.

He shrugs. "I thought it might be another prank, but it's just my mom's friend. Yesterday, someone rang the doorbell and left a box of ground beef on our front steps."

"Ground beef?" I repeat.

"In the shape of a brain. Get it? Because I like zombies?" He starts dusting his figurines a little more vigorously. "I'm going to set up a camera tonight so we can catch them next time."

"Wow, good luck," I say. As I keep dusting, I can't help thinking it's an awfully big coincidence that Andrew and I, the two shyest people in the eighth grade, are both having stupid pranks pulled on us. I don't know why Briana would single Andrew out, but I'm convinced it has to be her. Who else would get so much enjoyment out of making other people miserable?

Then I have an incredible thought: if Andrew manages to catch Briana on camera pulling one of her pranks, then maybe the Evil Queen will finally get what she deserves.

chapter 19

Mrs. Riley opens the door when we ring the bell. Her hair is perfectly fluffy, and there are so many pearls around her neck that they look like they might choke her.

"Oh good, you're here," she says. "We're having a dinner party tonight, so this place has to be spotless. And I need you to be gone before the caterer comes in an hour."

I can see where Briana gets her charming personality. I wonder if Evan takes after his father, or if he's just the black sheep of the family.

Mom is unfazed as usual. "Not a problem."

Mrs. Riley sighs. "I really need to just hire a housekeeper." Her rings sparkle as she picks up a shiny black purse. "I have to go out and run a few errands, but my husband is in his office down the hall, so you won't be alone." There's a warning tone in her voice, like she wants us to know that we won't have an opportunity to steal anything while she's gone.

"Enjoy the day!" Mom says cheerfully as Mrs. Riley hurries out the door. I don't know how she can stand being so nice to everyone. Then again, Mom works at a pretty fancy law firm, so she deals with snotty people all the time.

"I can do the bedrooms again," I say quickly.

"All right. But try to hurry."

I charge up the stairs armed with cleaning supplies, relieved that Evan isn't home. I don't think I could face him after yesterday's fiasco. Plus, snooping around Briana's room will be harder if he's nearby.

When I come to Evan's bedroom, I peek in, suddenly nervous for some reason.

Instead of a stereotypical messy boy room with band posters and piles of dirty laundry, Evan's room is covered with photographs of cool-looking buildings from all over the world, and there's an acoustic guitar at the foot of the bed. Evan even has a live fern on his windowsill. The last time I tried to keep a plant alive, it committed suicide by falling off the plant stand after only a day.

It feels like I'm intruding by being in Evan's room, but I remind myself that it's just my job and get to work. As I'm dusting the desk, I accidentally bump Evan's computer and the screen lights up. The wallpaper is of Evan, in a school uniform, with his arm around a cute girl who's also in uniform. Obviously his girlfriend.

It's stupid of me to feel disappointed. Evan is cute and smart. It figures he has a girlfriend. And anyway, why am I so bummed when Steve Mueller is literally the guy of my dreams?

I quickly finish up in Evan's room and head toward Briana's. I'm ready to start poking around as soon as I open the door, but when it swings open, I gasp. The entire carpet is covered in dirt. Not dirt that someone tracked in with muddy boots. This is dirt that's been evenly sprinkled over the whole floor.

As if I need a reminder that Briana Riley is a pumpkin-headed cow.

My chest sears with anger. And the worst part is, I have no choice but to clean up the mess or Mom and I will be in danger of losing this cleaning job, and maybe others. Word travels fast in town, and I don't want anyone hearing that we're bad at our jobs.

I grab the vacuum and start to suck up the dirt. It takes forever since I have to go over the carpet a few times to get rid of every speck, not to mention all the times I have to stop and empty the vacuum. As I work, I keep imaging

Briana Riley being swallowed up by a volcano or pecked to death by pigeons.

Finally, the carpet is done, and I hurry to clean every visible surface.

"Rachel, are you almost finished up there?" Mom calls up the stairs.

"One more minute!" If I'm going to search Briana's room, I have to do it now.

Holding my breath, I go over to her desk and pull open all the drawers. I expect to find some kind of incriminating evidence—love letters, for example. But there's nothing except the usual type of stuff: pens, markers, old quizzes. Nothing Steve Mueller would pay to hear about. I check under the mattress and behind the radiator. Finally, my eyes wander over to Briana's dresser.

I start from the bottom, pulling the drawers open one by one. As I look through endless rows of socks and pajamas, I'm amazed at how neatly each article of clothing is folded. But after meeting Mrs. Riley, I figure Briana can't get away with anything less.

Finally, I get to the top drawer, which has to be full of her underwear. I hesitate, not sure if I'm ready to cross that line. But if I'm going to find anything good, like a diary or something, it'll probably be in there. And if I do find a diary, think of all the secrets Steve Mueller might be willing to pay for. Heck, that could be my whole flight to Florida right there.

I take a deep breath and open the top drawer. I'm almost blinded by the white underwear beaming up at me. It all looks so satiny and lacy and expensive. No wonder she guffawed at the sight of my worn-out bra.

Before I lose my nerve, I plunge my hand in and start rifling around. And come up with…nothing. I open the drawer wider and search in the back, running my fingers along the edge. But still, there's nothing there except satiny underthings.

Frustrated, I start to shut the drawer, and that's when I hear footsteps in the hall. I shove the drawer closed the rest of the way just as Evan appears in the door, dressed in running clothes.

"Hi, Evan!" I chirp, probably sounding like a guilty blue jay.

"Hey," he says, giving me his usual crooked grin. My heart is still pounding, but Evan doesn't look suspicious. "I was hoping I might catch you before you go."

Wow. A guy has never looked forward to seeing me before. "You were?"

He takes a step toward me, and I smell the sweet scent of peppermint. "I'm really sorry about the way Kurt acted yesterday. He's such a jerk sometimes."

I can feel my shoulders sag. For a few minutes, at least, I'd forgotten all about stupid Kurt.

"I'm not even really friends with him," Evan goes on. "We just play baseball together. My actual friends are nice. I promise." He sounds so sincere that I can't help but relax. And anyway, he has a girlfriend, so it doesn't matter how I act. I'm not trying to impress him or anything.

"It's okay," I tell him.

"All right, I won't bother you while you're working. Everyone's been crazy because of this dinner party tonight for one of my dad's big clients. If something doesn't get done, it'll be my fault."

I smile. "So if I don't feel like cleaning something, I can just blame it on you?"

"Gee, thanks," he says. Then he gives me that grin of his one more time and goes down the hall to his room.

It takes me a good minute to get the fluttering in my stomach under control.

chapter 20

Finally, Mom and I come to our last house of the day. Ms. Montelle isn't home this time, so Caitlin silently lets us in and then goes right back to her spot on the couch. She's watching another one of my favorite cooking shows. It's an old episode I've never seen before, and I'd love to plop down on the floor and watch. But of course I have work to do. And being that close to Caitlin Schubert would probably set me on fire.

This time Mom sends me to do the bedrooms while she does the rest of the house. I start in Ms. Montelle's room, which is a mess of business suits and blouses thrown on top of every surface. I try to hang them up so I can actually clean the dressers and nightstands underneath.

When I'm done, I head across the hall to Caitlin's room, but she's standing in front of the closed door with her arms crossed in front of her chest.

"You're not allowed to come in here," she says.

"But—but we're supposed to clean the whole house." I can hear my mom whistling away in the bathroom. Should I try to get her help?

"No one's allowed in my room," Caitlin says. Then she stomps off down the hall and back to the living room.

I stand frozen for a minute, shocked that she finally spoke to me. Is there something in her room she doesn't want me to see? Or is she just being a jerk?

Either way, if she doesn't want us in there, then I guess we can't exactly kick the door down. With a shrug, I go toward the little office at the end of the hall.

As I finish dusting a beat-up desk in the far corner, I hear the front door of the house open and Ms. Montelle come in. She says something I can't hear to Caitlin and then calls out a quick hello to my mom before she goes into her bedroom and shuts the door.

I'm about to turn on the vacuum when I hear Ms. Montelle's muffled voice through the wall, clearly talking on the phone. I feel bad listening, but I can't help hearing every word.

"No, she's not doing okay. She refuses to leave the house except to go to school, and even that's been a struggle. All she does is sit around watching TV. It's been weeks since she saw any of her friends, even Briana. I'm afraid she's really getting depressed, but she won't go see the therapist the school counselor suggested. Can't you talk to her, Mother? She always listens to you."

Ms. Montelle falls silent, listening for a minute. I hold my breath, also listening.

"Of course I don't blame her for still being upset. Her father died! I know that's not something she can just get over. But Mother, she hardly knew the man. He hadn't seen her in years. I'm just not sure what to do to help her." There's another stretch of silence, and finally Ms. Montelle lets out a long sigh. "Okay, I'll call you tomorrow," she says before hanging up the phone.

I sit there totally stunned. Clearly, she'd been talking about Caitlin. Did her father really die? I think back to how weird Caitlin has been acting the past few weeks, barely talking, not really paying attention to Briana's usual antics. Now it all makes sense.

I can't imagine what she's going through. It must have been hard enough not seeing her father for years, but then to lose him all together? How totally horrible.

For the first time in my life, I actually feel bad for Caitlin Schubert. Maybe she isn't a heartless harpy after all.

chapter 21

The next day, Marisol comes over to help me do some serious stress baking while Mom is at her Sunday afternoon book group. My whole body aches from yesterday's cleaning marathon. Even my toes hurt. But a batch of comfort brownies will fix everything.

I decide to go all-out chocolate this time: chocolate chips, chocolate icing, and a sprinkle of M&M's. If that doesn't make me feel better, nothing will.

This would be the perfect time to tell Marisol about Steve Mueller paying me to spy on Briana, but I can't even imagine how she'll react. Instead, I fill her in on the previous day's events while we wait for the brownies to bake.

"I still can't believe it about Caitlin's father," says Marisol, carefully sorting through the M&M's to find all the red ones (her favorite).

"I never thought I'd feel bad for her, but I can't imagine

what she's going through." I shake my head. What would I do if I never saw my dad again?

I flip open my journal and turn to the last entry of the Dirt Diary. Writing Caitlin's secret down had felt wrong, but seeing it in writing also helped me process what had happened.

The timer goes off, and I jump up to pull the brownies out of the oven. As the hot air hits my face and mingles with the smell of chocolate, I don't feel quite so miserable anymore. Baking always has that effect on me.

After we let the brownies cool, Marisol and I start icing and sprinkling them with M&M's. When we're finished, the brownies look like cavities on a plate. I turn to the recipe section of my journal and make some notes about my latest creation. These days I barely use other people's recipes anymore. It's more fun to make up my own.

Finally, the brownies are cool enough to eat. I take a gooey bite, and the intense rush of chocolate and sugar warms me all the way down to my toes.

"Whoa," says Marisol. "I think I might have just gotten diabetes."

I laugh, realizing she's right. I might be in the mood

for death by chocolate, but maybe it's a little much. Yet another recipe that won't be making the bake sale cut.

"What's this?" says Marisol. She pulls over an old photo album that's sitting on the kitchen table.

"My mom found it during her latest cleaning tirade." I swallow a bite of brownie before adding, "She's been emptying out all the closets in case we can't keep the house."

Marisol's mouth falls open. "You guys wouldn't move out of town, would you?"

Oh my goldfish. I hadn't even thought of that. I assumed if we had to move, we'd stay in town. "I'd die if I had to start over at a new school," I say. "All those new people. I don't think I could handle it."

It took six whole years of school before Marisol saw through my shyness and wanted to be friends with me. I can't be an outcast like that again. I must've been delusional when I tried to convince Dad to let me move to Florida with him. It hadn't occurred to me that moving would have meant starting my whole life over.

"It'll be okay," Marisol says, giving me a sympathetic smile. "If you had to move, I'd find a way to come over every day."

"Thanks." I don't know what I'd do without Marisol. She's the only person keeping me sane most of the time.

"Oh my gosh!" Marisol squeals, looking through the pictures from when I was little. "I love this one."

She points to a photo of me and Dad wearing matching reindeer ears and holding ice cubes on our outstretched tongues. It was taken at Mom's company holiday party when I was in third grade. I was too afraid to talk to anyone, so Dad made up all kinds of funny games for the two of us to play while Mom spent the evening schmoozing with coworkers.

So many other memories of Dad and me come rushing back that I have to look away.

"You were so cute," says Marisol. She looks up. "And you still are. That's why I'm sure there's someone much better out there for you than stupid Steve Mueller. Briana Riley can have him."

I bite into my brownie again, trying to distract myself from the thought buzzing around in my head: now that I've taken Steve up on his offer, maybe he'll ditch the Evil Queen and finally notice me.

chapter 22

As I'm making curry tuna casserole that night—Dad's favorite—my cell phone rings. I grab it just as the oven finishes preheating.

"Hello?" I say, shoving the pan into the oven at the same time.

"Is this Rachel?" a guy's voice asks.

"Um, yes?"

"Hey, it's Steve. Steve Mueller."

I almost fall into the oven. Steve Mueller is calling me! On the phone!

"Listen," he goes on. "I was wondering if you'd had a chance to look around Briana's room. You know, for what we talked about?"

"Um. Uh-huh." I shut the oven door and stumble over to the kitchen table, feeling slightly dizzy.

"So, did you find anything?" he asks.

"Er." If I tell him the truth, then it'll all be over. No extra money to put back in my college fund. And, more importantly, no Steve Mueller calling me! "Well," I squeak. "I did find…a note." Did I really just say that? Of course, it sounded totally unconvincing. There's no way in Helena, Montana, he'll believe it.

"Who was it from?"

"It—it wasn't signed. But it was in…her math book."

"What did it say?"

"Uh, something like, 'I can't wait to see you again.' It looked like a guy's handwriting." Whoa, what am I doing?

I can hear Steve breathing into the phone. This is it. He'll get mad and decide to confront Briana about it. She'll deny the whole thing, and they'll have a huge fight, and the two of them will break up. She deserves it, I remind myself. She's the one who's gone out of her way to make my life miserable. Once Steve dumps her, he'll come running into my arms while cheesy music plays in the background. Maybe he'll even ask me to the Spring Dance. Or…he'll realize that I lied to him and never speak to me again.

"Oh," Steve says finally. The weird thing is, he doesn't sound mad. He just sounds kind of hurt. Is it possible he has real feelings for Briana? "Well, thanks for telling me. I'll make sure to pay you tomorrow in school."

"Wait. Are you going to tell Briana what I told you?"

"No. I don't think an unsigned note is much to go on. If you don't mind, I'll still have you keep an eye out."

"Oh, okay." I can't help it. Even though I feel like rat dandruff for lying, I'm still excited that I'll get to talk to him again, have a chance to earn more money, and get back at Briana, all at the same time. Still, he sounds so miserable. "I wouldn't worry about the note," I say. "It probably doesn't mean anything."

Steve lets out a sad little laugh. "It's funny. I kept telling myself that I wanted to find out she was cheating on me because that would explain the way she's been acting. But I guess I'd really been hoping it was something else." Then, before I can confess that I made it all up, he hangs up the phone, and I'm alone to face my guilty conscience. I have a feeling it's going to punch me right in the face.

chapter 23

At school on Monday morning, I find a crisp twenty-dollar bill in my locker. As I put it in my bag, I can't help feeling slimy. But the thought that the money was once in Steve Mueller's pocket makes my insides tingle. Yes, I'm totally pathetic.

The money puts me at just about $100, and I still have two weeks until Mom finds out what I've done. If I save every cent between now and then, and if I manage to win the bake-sale competition this year, my whole crazy plan just might work.

As I flip through my cooking journal in homeroom, I watch Caitlin out of the corner of my eye. How did I not notice before how terrible she looks? Her skin is pale and gray, her hair looks like it's never seen a brush, and she's wearing sweatpants to school. Sweatpants! She and Briana used to be identical rich twins, but now next to Briana, Caitlin looks like a bag lady.

The Dirt Diary

I want to go over and tell her how sorry I am about her dad, to ask if there's anything I can do to make her feel better, but that would mean admitting that I'd been eavesdropping on her mom's phone conversation. And anyway, I'm probably the last person she wants sympathy from.

Briana, however, doesn't seem to notice anything different about Caitlin. She's talking to her just like she always does. Or *at* her.

"So since I'm head of the Spring Dance committee this year, I think we need to go all out. I mean we only have two weeks left to plan, and it has to be really special. It's like our last chance to leave our middle-school legacy," Briana is saying before Social Studies class. Meanwhile, Caitlin is just doodling in her notebook, not doing a very good job of pretending to pay attention. At one point she glances over at Steve Mueller, and they exchange something like a knowing smile, like they both see how ridiculous Briana is. Steve might be upset about the possibility of Briana cheating on him, but maybe he isn't blind to her faults after all.

"What are you staring at?" Briana snaps, whirling toward me. I practically jump out of my seat. "Do I have a piece of dirt on my face or something? You want to clean it, don't you? You just can't help yourself."

I imagine what it would feel like to cut her ponytail off with garden shears. I can almost hear that satisfying *snip*.

Angela Bareli giggles in the row next to us. "Briana," she says in her high, nasally voice, "did I tell you I saw a vacuum cleaner in Rachel's locker?"

Briana clicks her tongue. "Doesn't surprise me. That thing's her new boyfriend. She dumped Troy to date it." She laughs and so does almost everyone else in the class. I don't dare look to see if Steve is one of them.

When I'm at my locker after lunch, I spot Marisol charging toward me, her eyes narrowed and her cheeks flushed. Uh-oh. She must have found out about my deal with Steve Mueller somehow.

"Hi, Marisol," I say over my shoulder as I open my locker and pretend to look for something.

"I was talking to Angela Bareli on the bus this morning."

"Since when do you talk to her? I thought you said she's a total follower." I'm stalling, and we both know it.

"She's not so bad once you get to know her, but that's not important," says Marisol. "What matters is what she told me. She said she saw you—"

I close my eyes, ready for Marisol to start lecturing me on my lack of morality. But she suddenly falls quiet. When

I open my eyes, I see she's facing away from me, looking at someone in the middle of the hallway. It's Andrew Ivanoff. His ears, as usual, are burning with embarrassment.

"Hello, Rachel," he half-whispers, his eyes just barely meeting mine.

"Hi, Andrew," I answer. "Um, what's up?"

"I just wanted to thank you. For your suggestion. About putting people in my movie. It helped."

"Oh. Good." I don't think the idea of putting people in a zombie movie is that revolutionary, but I'm glad it helped him get unstuck with his screenplay. "How's the movie going?"

"Very well, in fact. I've been scouting locations and found the perfect field for the final battle scene. The grass is so tall, it'll almost swallow up the toys. I think it'll look very dramatic." His voice is more animated than I've ever heard it.

Marisol is looking back and forth between us like we're a ping-pong match.

"Oh," I say. "Andrew, this is my friend Marisol. She lives down the street from you."

"I know," he answers, giving Marisol the briefest of smiles. "We ride the same bus. You always sit in the left row of seats."

"I guess I do. Well, it's nice to officially meet you," says Marisol. But Andrew is already rushing away like he might explode from mortification at any moment. "See ya," Marisol calls after him. She turns back to me. "What a strange guy."

"Yup. But now you can say you've met a filmmaker, right?"

She smiles. Then her face falls like she's remembered why she stormed over to me in the first place. But at that moment the bell rings.

"Sorry, gotta go!" I say, slamming my locker shut.

Marisol catches my arm. "We have to talk. My house tonight, okay?"

I sigh. So much for making a getaway. "Fine. See you tonight."

chapter 24

I convince my mom to drop me off at Marisol's house on her way to a PTA meeting. She's usually not thrilled about me going anywhere on a school night, but she seems distracted today.

"Are you okay, Mom?" I ask as we pull into Marisol's neighborhood.

"I'm fine," she answers, twisting her wedding band around her finger. "Just tired."

It's like someone took one of our regular conversations and reversed it. Since when am I the concerned one and Mom the quiet one? Next thing you know, I'll be telling her to have some confidence in herself.

"Rachel," she says after a minute. "Did you tell Mr. Hammond that your father was coming back?"

I blink at her. I'd forgotten about my little outburst the other night. "Um, maybe?" I expect her to look mad, but instead she just lets out a long sigh like she's disappointed in me.

"Why would you say that? You know it's not true."

Because I don't want Mr. Hammond thinking he can start hitting on my mom. Because I'm not willing to accept that Dad is never coming back. And a million other reasons, none of which I can say in a way that won't make Mom go ballistic.

"I–I don't know," I say instead.

"I understand things have been hard without your father around, but we've been managing on our own, haven't we?" Her voice is soft and hesitant, like she's afraid I might disagree with her.

"It's just…Dad's changed his mind about stuff before. Remember when he got his real estate license and then he decided he didn't want to change careers after all?" I cringe, realizing that I've just reminded Mom how impulsive my dad can be. "I just mean, don't you think he might realize he's made a huge mistake and come back?"

Mom slowly shakes her head. "I don't think so. Not when it comes to this." We pull up in front of Marisol's house. "All right, I'll be back in an hour or two," she says, her voice back to its usual volume. It's clear she doesn't want to talk about my dad anymore.

When I get out of the minivan, Marisol's front door swings open. I swallow, feeling like I'm entering a dragon's lair as I go meet her at the doorway.

"Come on upstairs," she says without her usual greeting smile.

When we get to her room, she rushes over to her desk to turn on some music. Yup, that means a boy-related conversation. Marisol's mom wants her to save dating for when she's older, so any talk about boys has to be conducted in whispers. This, of course, goes against Marisol's policy of always being honest about things, but when it comes to boys, she's willing to make an exception.

"Angela Bareli said she saw you talking to Steve Mueller in the hallway last week," she says, pulling me over to sit on the bed.

"Um, yeah, I talked to him." I look down at her cranberry-colored carpet. "He just wanted to ask me something."

"And you didn't tell me! Well, what did he say to you?"

I swallow. Now that she's flat-out asked me about it, I can't just lie to her face.

"Rach?" Marisol says, looking me right in the eyes.

I'm powerless. "He asked me to spy on Briana."

"He *what*?"

"It's not a big deal. It's just that he's afraid she might be cheating on him. He wanted me to keep an eye out and let him know if I heard or saw anything suspicious."

"What a slimeball!"

Okay, that's crossing the line. "He's not a slimeball! Briana's the one who's a big ball of slime. She's the one who might be cheating on him."

"If he has someone spying for him, then he deserves to be cheated on," says Marisol. Why does she always expect that everyone will be as honest and perfect as she is? "You're not going to do it, are you?"

I don't dare look her in the eye.

"Ray-chul?" She draws my name out the same way Mom does when I'm in trouble. "Tell me you're not really considering spying on Briana."

It's no use lying. Marisol can always drag the truth out of me. "You don't have to try to talk me out of it," I mumble. "Because I already did."

"You *what*?" Marisol cries, acting like I just told her I murdered somebody.

I know what I did wasn't exactly moral, but after everything Briana has done to me, is it really so bad?

"It's just a way for me to make some more money to put back in my college fund."

"So let me get this straight," Marisol shoots back at me. "You're getting paid to spy on someone so you can replace the cash you *stole*?"

It sounds bad when she puts it like that, but doesn't she understand that I have no choice? No, she doesn't, because her parents are still together and can pay for anything she wants.

"You don't get it, okay? You don't need money the way I do. If I can go to Florida and bring my dad back, then it'll all be worth it."

"Even if it means doing things you know are totally wrong?"

"Yes!" I jump to my feet, something inside me breaking loose. "I'm not scamming innocent people or anything. This is Briana Riley we're talking about. Why can't I make money off someone who's been so horrible to me?"

"Because then you're just as bad as she is!" says Marisol. "What are you going to do next? Start selling the secrets you've been writing in that diary of yours?"

"Of course not!"

She shakes her head like she doesn't believe me. "Maybe

I don't have to worry about money like you do, but that doesn't mean I'm a spoiled brat. And I'm sick of you acting like you're some kind of victim!"

"When do I act like that?" We're face-to-face now, yelling at each other for the first time ever in our friendship.

"All the time! Whenever anyone says the slightest thing to you, you act like your life is over. 'Poor me, people make fun of me.' That's why Briana won't leave you alone, because you're an easy target. And the only reason Steve Mueller asked you to spy on her is because he knew you would do whatever he said. You need to grow a spine, Rachel!"

"*You* grow a spine!" Comebacks have never been my thing.

"And this whole thing with your parents. Do you honestly believe you can get them back together? That's the dumbest thing I've ever heard!"

I can't breathe. Did my best friend really just say that to me?

When my mouth opens, my tongue's turned into a knife. "Oh yeah? Well, you need to face facts too. Your clothes suck, and everyone knows it. No one will ever want to wear that crap."

Marisol steps back like I just punched her in the stomach.

Instantly, I regret what I said. It's not true, not at all. But it's too late to take it back.

I can feel the tears stinging at my eyes. The last thing I want is to prove how spineless I am by bawling like a baby, so I push past Marisol and tear out of the house.

chapter 25

The sun is setting over the trees as I trudge through Marisol's neighborhood, the light hitting me right in the eyes. I have no idea where I'm going, and I know Mom will be coming to pick me up soon. But I can't face Marisol again, so I just keep going and going. Why does it feel like I'm always running away on the verge of an emotional meltdown lately?

Finally, I stop at the corner and plop down on the curb. There are lights on inside the houses across the street, and I can see shadows of people walking around and watching TV. None of them care that Marisol and I just had a screaming fight.

What she said swirls in my head. *Am* I a terrible person for agreeing to spy on Briana? Not only that, but I lied to Steve Mueller about it too.

But Marisol is wrong about my parents. I know they

still care about each other. There has to be a way to get them back together, there just has to be. Otherwise...it means my family is really gone.

I'm pulled out of my mopey thoughts by the sound of approaching footsteps. At first I think it's Marisol coming after me, but then I realize the feet are wearing sneakers instead of heels. I turn to see Evan Riley jogging toward me. He's dressed in basketball shorts and a faded T-shirt, his hair wet with perspiration.

I duck my head, hoping he won't notice me and just run by, but he's already slowing down.

"Hey, Booger Crap," he says, smiling. "I didn't know you were on my running route." Even with beads of sweat glistening on his forehead he's still super cute.

"Hey," I mumble.

His smile fades. "Are you okay?"

I start to say I'm fine, but what comes out of my mouth is: "My best friend and I just had a huge fight."

"Oh, I'm sorry. You want to talk about it?"

There's no way Evan wants to hear about my problems, and I'm not sure I want to rehash what just happened. "No, that's okay."

Evan shrugs. "Do you mind if I sit down?"

I don't want him to see me like this, but I realize that I don't want him to leave either. Having Evan here is better than being alone with my depressing thoughts.

"Sure."

He smiles and perches on the curb nearby, close enough that I can feel the heat radiating off him. "So are you working with your mom to save up for something?" he asks.

I nod.

"Anything good?"

"I hope so," I say. And before I know it, I'm telling him about my parents splitting up and about me going down to Florida. I leave out the part about lying and cheating my way to get there, but I tell him about my plan to try to get my parents back together. I even tell him about seeing the taping of *Pastry Wars* with my dad. The words just pour out of me like they *need* to be said.

When I'm done, I expect Evan to make an excuse and run away. I mean, what guy wants to deal with all that drama? But instead he nods slowly and says, "Wow. That's rough about your parents. I hope your plan works."

"Yeah, me too. My mom's been acting so weird. I'm afraid she's starting to really lose it." This is the first time I've told anyone about how bad things have gotten with my mom.

Even Marisol only knows the bare minimum. I've been too embarrassed, and too scared, to tell anyone the truth before, but for some reason talking to Evan is easy.

"Your mom seems all right to me," he says, "but I don't know her that well. I bet she'll be okay once things calm down, though."

"I hope you're right." I'm still convinced that the best way to get my mom back to normal is to bring Dad home, but it makes me feel better that Evan doesn't think she's nutso.

"I can't believe you're going to see *Pastry Wars*," Evan says, looking over at me. "I love that show."

"You do?"

"I watch it whenever it's on TV, even reruns. Did you see the one where they had to make baklava?"

"Yes! I couldn't believe the guy put candied honeybees on top as a garnish!"

"So gross," he says, scrunching up his nose. "I don't care if you do take the stinger out. There's no way I'd eat a bee."

"I know! Did you see the one with the frogs?"

"That's one of my favorite episodes!"

We laugh about a few other crazy pastry concoctions before Evan turns to me and says, "Hey, I think new episodes are coming back on soon. We should watch them together."

"That would be fun."

"Cool. We'll have to make a plan," he says just as my mom's car pulls up in front of us.

"There you are," Mom calls out the car window. "Marisol said you ran off. I've been driving around looking for you."

I jump to my feet, realizing it's almost dark out. "Sorry," I say. Mom's face has that pinched look that means she's annoyed. The last thing I want is to get yelled at in front of Evan.

"All right. Hop in," she says. "We'll talk about this at home."

Relieved, I turn back to Evan. Despite the fact that we were just chatting like old friends a minute ago, I suddenly feel awkward around him again.

"Well, it was nice to run into you," he says.

I nod.

"I'll see you on Saturday?"

I nod again. Why won't my tongue just work? I force myself to say something, anything. "Good luck," I blurt out.

Evan looks surprised. "Thanks?" Then he smiles his little crooked smile, waves at my mom, and starts to jog away.

Only after I'm in Mom's car do I realize something. Did Evan Riley just ask me out on a date? No, that's impossible. Isn't it?

chapter 26

Marisol sits quietly in the corner in homeroom the next day, doodling in her sketch pad. She glances up at me a couple times but quickly looks away. I know she's waiting for me to go over and apologize, and to tell her she's right and that I should've never agreed to be Steve Mueller's spy. But can't she see that I have no choice? And there are things I want to hear Marisol apologize for too. If she isn't going to make the first move, then I'm not either.

Instead, I take out my Dirt Diary and start pouring my heart out. What started out as a log of cleaning jobs has quickly morphed into a mishmash of crazy ideas and observations, essentially all the things I can't tell anyone else. The thought makes me feel even more alone.

Needless to say, I'm in a foul mood when I leave homeroom and head off to English. But that all changes when

I spot Steve Mueller in the hallway. He's walking toward me, like he has a million times before, but this time he actually looks at me instead of looking through me. And even though he doesn't say anything, he smiles at me as he passes by. Steve Mueller smiled at me! In public!

The giddiness only lasts for about an hour, until I see Marisol again in Chemistry class. She and Angela Bareli are huddled together like they have some serious BFF secrets to share. Looking at them makes my teeth clench.

As I head to gym class later in the day, I'm lost in a jumble of thoughts, so it takes me a second to realize that someone's calling my name.

I turn to see Andrew Ivanoff waving at me, his pale hair shielding his eyes.

"Um, hi," I say, going over to him.

"Um, hi," he echoes.

Wow, aren't we the chatty duo.

"Have you started filming yet?" I finally ask.

He shakes his head. "That's why I wanted to speak with you. You've been so helpful. I was hoping…" He pauses and looks at his hands, like human speech has failed him.

"What's the problem?"

"The zombies are ready, but I'm having trouble with the

costumes for the people. I don't know much about how kids our age dress."

I take in Andrew's outfit. Pressed khakis, striped button-down shirt, brown loafers. He's pretty much dressed like my dad.

"I know the perfect person to help you," I say, ready to tell him all about Marisol's fashion skills. Then I remember that she and I aren't speaking to each other. "Me. I can help you."

"You can?" Andrew asks, clearly checking out my nondescript outfit.

"Okay, I may not be a fashion guru, but I know enough to make your movie people look like real people. If you want, I can help you brainstorm ideas on Saturday when my mom and I come by."

He nods, and there's even something like a smile on his face. "Thank you. You're really nice," he says. Then he walks away, and I can see that the back of his neck is flushed red.

As I go to change into my gym clothes, I realize that Andrew is wrong about me. It's been days, maybe even weeks, since I've felt like a nice person.

chapter 27

On Saturday, I'm actually excited to go to the Rileys' house since it means seeing Evan again. So I can't help feeling disappointed when his mother informs us that he had to go play golf with his father after Mr. Riley's usual partner injured his foot. And I can't even snoop around Briana's room again because she's home and refuses to let me into her room. "I don't want that stalker in here," she tells her mother.

It's a relief when we go to Andrew Ivanoff's house. I'll take zombies over Briana any day. The camera is still set up over the front door, which I guess means they haven't found the prank culprits yet. I have an amazing mental image of Briana behind bars, in one of those old-timey black-and-white prison outfits. If only…

After we finish cleaning the Ivanoffs' house, I go upstairs to see Andrew while my mom gets our stuff together. His room is a much more controlled mess than the last time I saw it. The zombie toys are all lined up in tight rows on Andrew's desk, while the model of the school is right in the middle of his room. He asked us not to clean in here today since he's afraid we might mess everything up.

"What do you think?" he says, pointing to a pile of Barbies. "I have the whole popular crowd."

As I study Barbie, Ken, and their various friends, I recognize ones that look a lot like Steve Mueller, Briana Riley, and Caitlin Schubert. Andrew did an amazing job of finding dolls to play them.

"So these are the humans in your movie?" I ask, tugging on the Briana doll's hair. "I hope everyone gets killed by zombies at the end." I glance at the Ken that's clearly supposed to be Steve Mueller. Well, maybe not everyone.

Andrew's face falls. "I knew my ending was too predictable!"

"Wait, they really all die at the end?"

"Of course. It's completely unrealistic to think humans could survive when there's such widespread zombie-ism."

"That's a creepy thought," I say.

"These are the clothes I found." Steve holds up some typical Barbie outfits that probably looked dated even before the toys were out of their packaging. Marisol could have taken a scrap of fabric and somehow fashioned an entire wardrobe out of it, but I'll just have to do the best I can on my own.

"I guess we could alter some of their clothes to make them look more modern," I say.

Andrew nods. Then he looks down at his carpet like there's something written on it. "I haven't seen you with your friend Marisol recently."

"Oh." I swallow, thinking of all the times I've watched Marisol hanging out with Angela the past few days. "We had a fight. I'm not sure we're even friends anymore."

"Because of one argument?"

"It wasn't just an argument," I say, smoothing down a Barbie dress. "We both said things that are...hard to take back."

Andrew nods slowly, like he's considering what I said. "Well, I hope you find a way to work it out."

"Me too. I should probably get going. My mom's waiting for me in the car." I start gathering up the dolls, but Andrew stops me.

"Wait." His cheeks turn a deep shade of red. It's a wonder he has blood left anywhere else in his body. "Listen, I was wondering...It's okay if you say no..." He opens his mouth like he's gulping air, which only makes me nervous.

"What?" I finally say.

"Well, I wondered if you'd maybe…want to go to the Spring Dance…with me."

A Ken falls out of my hand and lands on the floor with a thud. "The Spring Dance?"

"It's okay if you don't want to. I understand."

"No, it's not that," I say. "It's just, we don't really know each other that well."

"It would be as friends," says Andrew. "I just…don't know a lot of girls. And I think we'd have fun."

In all my wild fantasies about guys asking me out (most of them starring Steve Mueller), I never dreamed that a zombie-loving filmmaker would ask me to the Spring Dance. But Andrew is a nice guy, even if he is kind of odd, and I'm totally flattered he'd ask me.

"Sure, I'll go with you."

"You will?" Andrew glances up at me, and there's an actual smile on his face. "My parents will be so happy I found a date. They're constantly telling me I need to be more social."

"My mom's always saying the same thing."

After I leave Andrew's house, I desperately want to run over to Marisol's house and tell her about all the crazy things that have happened to me: Evan maybe asking me on a date, Andrew asking me to the dance. But I have to remind myself that Marisol doesn't care. She and Angela are probably sitting out on Angela's porch together, having a great time.

The realization that I have so much news and no one to tell it to makes my excitement deflate. Practically overnight, I've gone back to what life was like before Marisol and I became friends.

Everything feels so bottled up inside me that when I get into Mom's minivan, I find myself announcing: "I'm going to the Spring Dance!"

Mom glances over at me. "Say that again?"

"Andrew Ivanoff asked me to the Spring Dance."

"How nice. I'm sure you two will have a great time." Okay, it's not exactly the enthusiasm I was looking for.

"Aren't you surprised that someone would actually ask me to the dance? I bet you would've never predicted this."

"Well, I guess it's a bit unexpected, but why would I be surprised that someone would want to go with you?"

I roll my eyes. "Mom, it's sweet that you don't think I'm a loser, but everyone else does."

"Rachel, what have I told you about using that word? If

you think of yourself as a loser, then people will treat you like you are one."

Right, and this is why I never talk to my mom about stuff. She's convinced that any problem can be fixed with determination (and a good spring cleaning). And it's also why I can never tell her about Briana sprinkling her entire room with dirt for me to clean up. The last thing I need is Mom sitting me and Briana down and trying to get us to talk things out. Briana is just one of those people you can't reason with.

I'm quiet for the rest of the car ride, thinking about Evan Riley and Steve Mueller and Andrew Ivanoff. My life has become crazier since Mom started her cleaning business, but it's also filled with a lot more boys. I just wish I still had my best friend to share it with.

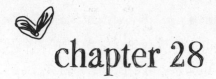

chapter 28

At school on Monday, it feels like everything around me has new meaning. I watch Caitlin Schubert flipping absently through a book and Steve Mueller staring out the window, while Briana goes on and on about decorations for the Spring Dance. When I glance at Marisol, hunched over some homework, I can't help thinking about all the changes in my life that she has no idea about.

But the thing I most want to change, my parents' relationship, is starting to feel completely out of my reach. I have less than two weeks left, and my peanut butter jar only has $124.25 in it. If I don't win the bake sale competition, it's back to the nursing home for me. And this time, I have a feeling Mom will make sure I'm put on bedpan duty.

I spend most of lunch poring over my journal, trying to figure out the perfect bake-sale recipe, but still no luck. I'm tempted to freak out, but I don't have time for meltdowns.

Instead, I flip to the end and fill up more pages of the Dirt Diary. I jot down all the odd things I noticed on Saturday, including Andrew's popular-kid dolls. For once, our visit to Caitlin's house was uneventful since she spent the whole time in her room. Hopefully, things will stay that way from now on.

At the end of the day, I go to my locker only to find it full of gummy worms. Fabulous. It must have taken Briana forever to push them in through the vents. Most of the worms are easy to clean up, but a few have started to melt, which means that my math book is now sticky and strawberry-scented.

I'm fuming so much that I consider going to Mr. Hammond and telling him what happened. But I have no proof that Briana was the one who did it, and even if he did believe me, I'm afraid he'd tell my mom and then she'd go into fix-it mode. Which would just make everything worse.

By the time I'm finished cleaning my locker, my bus is long gone. As I leave the school and walk past the softball field, I'm glad the team has an away game today. I definitely can't handle the sight of Briana Riley. I might just snap and start stuffing gummy worms down her throat.

Since the weather finally feels like spring, I don't rush

home. Instead, I enjoy the warm breeze on my face and try to take those deep, cleansing breaths Mom is always suggesting. After a while, I actually start to feel better. Yes, I'm still furious at Briana, but if these stupid pranks are the best she can come up with, then she's seriously pathetic.

When I get to Main Street, I stroll along looking into shop windows. I can't help thinking about Marisol. Maybe this whole fight we're having is stupid. I don't even feel all that mad anymore. I just miss her.

I decide to cross the street and peek into Second Dressed. Marisol loves hanging out there after school. Maybe there's a chance she's there now.

When I first peer through the store window, there doesn't seem to be anyone inside, and a balloon of disappointment wells up inside me. Then I spot someone in the far corner of the store, standing in front of a full-length mirror. It's Marisol, decked out in a long, turquoise gown.

I'm about to hurry into the store and tell her how sorry I am when I realize she's not alone. Angela Bareli is with her, and they're doing an ugly montage, laughing and chatting like they've been friends their whole lives.

My stomach starts churning. I can't believe it. Am I really that replaceable? I rush away before either of them sees me.

All I want is to go home and hole up in my room until this stupid day is over. But when I get back to the house, I'm surprised to see Mom's minivan parked outside.

As I open the door, I hear laughter coming from the kitchen.

"Robert, you're too much!" Mom says, still laughing.

Holy butternut squash. It's Mr. Hammond. I want to back out the door and make a run for it, but it's too late.

"Rachel, is that you?" Mom calls, as if it could be anyone else. "Come on in here."

I have no choice. When I go into the kitchen, Mom is sitting at the table while Mr. Hammond, dressed in a purple apron, is enthusiastically peeling a mound of potatoes.

"Hi there!" he says, sounding like he's genuinely glad to see me. "Your mother confessed that she's never had potato pancakes, so I'm making you gals some."

"Isn't that great?" says Mom.

I'm shocked to see that the kitchen's a total wreck compared to how Mom usually keeps it. There's even a dirty mixing bowl on the kitchen table. Apparently, Mr. Hammond is the only person allowed to make a mess.

"What are you doing home?" I ask.

"Robert left work a little early today, and he convinced me to do the same," Mom says. "I needed a bit of a break."

Seeing Mom there laughing with Mr. Hammond makes me furious. I just want to say something, anything, to make her feel miserable too. "Will your boss pay you for the time off?"

Mom's smile falters. "It won't make much of a difference."

"I thought you said we needed to make as much money as we could and save up every penny."

"I'd say your mom works plenty hard enough," says Mr. Hammond.

I ignore him and keep my eyes locked on Mom. "So that's it, then. You're just going to give up on Dad?"

Her eyes get really wide. "What are you talking about?"

"He's only been gone a few weeks, and you're already moving on, pretending like he doesn't exist anymore?"

Mom gets to her feet and comes over to me. "Rachel," she says in a low voice, "we can talk about this later, when it's just the two of us."

But the words burning inside of me can't wait another second. "You don't even care that he's gone, do you? You don't care that our family's fallen apart and that my entire life is ruined. All you care about is your new business and your new life without Dad!"

"Rachel, stop it. That's not true."

"Then why are you doing this? Why can't you at least try to make things work?"

"Your father is the one who left us, not the other way around! He's the one who abandoned this family. He's the one who gave up on it. If there's anyone you should be yelling at, it's him!"

"That's not fair—" I start to say, but Mom cuts me off.

"I don't want to talk about this anymore, Rachel. Not now. Go to your room and stay there until you've calmed down."

"Then I'll stay in there forever because I'll never be okay with this!" I rush past Mr. Hammond and into my room.

As I flop on my bed, my body pulses with hatred and anger and all the other things that lead to the dark side. I can feel the tears burning at my throat, but I'm sick of crying. It feels like that's all I've been doing for weeks. Really, for my whole life.

chapter 29

On my way to first period the next morning, I'm surprised to see Mr. Hammond waving to me from the end of the hallway. After my breakdown in front of him and my mom yesterday, I would think he'd be avoiding me. For a second, I consider pretending I don't see him, but then he'll just find me somewhere else.

As Mr. Hammond walks toward me, I suddenly remember the diapers I found in his bathroom, and I can't help looking down at his pants. My face ignites, but as he comes closer, I can't look away. Are his pants bulging? Are they unnaturally saggy? They look normal, but maybe adult diapers are thin enough that you don't notice them. I'm totally hypnotized.

By the time Mr. Hammond is standing in front of me, I've gone from spellbound to mortified.

"I was hoping I'd run into you," he says. "I found

something I thought you might be interested in." He holds out a flyer from one of the bakeries in town. "They're offering a pastry-making class over the summer. I thought it sounded right up your alley. And it's cheaper than the classes at the college."

I stare down at the flyer. Okay, so Mr. Hammond is obviously trying to get in good with me because he's interested in Mom. But I have to admit the class sounds amazing, even if I won't be able to take it. If all goes well, I'll be in Florida with Dad.

"Thanks," I say. "But I don't think—"

"I mentioned it to your mother before you came home yesterday, and she seemed open to the idea."

I look up at him. "She did?" Considering how much she complains about me spending too much time cooking and not enough studying, I would think she'd shoot it down right away. Not to mention the cost. Of course, now that she's mad at me, she's probably changed her mind.

"Maybe one of these days you'll wind up with a cooking show of your own," says Mr. Hammond.

The thought of me standing in front of a TV camera and talking to thousands of people is so ridiculous that I actually laugh.

Mr. Hammond smiles. "I think that's the happiest I've ever seen you look." He walks away, whistling, and it's all I can do not to stare at his butt.

I realize, suddenly, that I'm not the only one who's interested in the vice principal's behind. A cluster of girls near me are looking at Mr. Hammond and giggling. I swear I hear the word "diaper" in their whispered conversation.

I must be imagining things. No one else could know about my discovery.

But when I get to first period, I hear Briana and a few of her followers gossiping in the back of the room, and for once it isn't about me.

"I bet he wears them so he can just walk around the school all day looking for troublemakers without ever having to take a bathroom break," one of Steve's friends is saying.

Briana snorts. "Or maybe he's just ancient. My grandfather had to wear them, and he was like eighty when he died." Leave it to Briana to laugh about a deceased relative.

But the worst part is that when I sit down, I spot Marisol on the edge of Briana's group, right next to Angela Bareli. Even though Marisol isn't laughing like everyone else, she's still acting like she's always belonged to the popular crowd.

That's when I realize Marisol is the one who told everyone about the diapers in Mr. Hammond's bathroom after I swore her to secrecy. I don't need more proof that she and I aren't friends anymore.

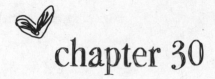

chapter 30

I spend the next couple days in a fog. Mom and I are barely speaking to each other, especially since she's been talking to Mr. Hammond for hours on the phone every night. The one good thing is that she's been less focused on organizing things lately, but I still have to un-alphabetize my books on an almost daily basis.

Meanwhile, all anyone at school can talk about (besides Mr. Hammond's bathroom habits) is the Spring Dance. I should be thrilled to be going, but I feel totally lost.

Normally, I'd have Marisol help me find a dress, but now that she and Angela are attached at the hip, that isn't an option. Plus, I can't afford to buy a dress. I have a boring black-and-white one I wore to my cousin's wedding that kind of makes me look like a nun. It will have to do. I only hope Andrew isn't too embarrassed to be seen with me.

I have a week and a half before Mom finds out about the

money. Even after we clean Mr. Hammond's and a couple other houses tonight, I'll be more than a hundred dollars short. So much is riding on the bake sale competition that thinking about it makes me feel sick, especially since I keep hearing about the top-secret new recipe Angela Bareli will be using this year,

"Are you all right?" Ms. Kennedy asks when I show up in the Home Ec room for the third day in a row during lunchtime. It's way better than eating at a table by myself. "I don't mind having you here, of course, but you don't usually come down so often."

Since I can't exactly ask her for cash or to help me fix all the messes I've gotten myself into, I just shrug and say, "I'm trying to figure out a recipe for the bake sale." While this is technically true, Ms. Kennedy doesn't look convinced. Luckily, she doesn't pry.

I'm still in a haze at the end of the school day when I'm on my way to catch the bus. So I don't even notice my mom standing in the school lobby until she starts waving at me.

I know something has to be wrong. My mind is spinning as I hurry over to her. "Is Dad okay?"

Mom blinks at me, clearly confused. "I think so. Why?"

"You never come pick me up." I don't add that it's especially strange given how little she's been speaking to me recently. Maybe she's finally forgiven me for yelling at her in front of Mr. Hammond.

"Of course I do," she says. "My boss didn't need me this afternoon, so I thought I'd swing by and save you a bus trip home."

I'm about to press my luck and ask if we can stop to get ice cream on the way when Mom glances past me and smiles. I look over my shoulder in time to see Mr. Hammond coming out of the main office. The minute he catches sight of Mom, a huge grin spreads across his face.

"I'll be right back, honey," Mom says before practically prancing over to him. I can't believe it. Mom isn't here to pick me up or to make amends. She's here to see him! Apparently, she couldn't wait until tonight.

My chest feels like it's full of lava as Mom throws her head back and laughs at something Mr. Hammond is saying, her hand resting on his arm.

"Oh my god," someone says from behind me. "Why is my cleaning lady hanging all over my vice principal?"

Of course, it's Briana. The usual crowd of followers all laugh except for Caitlin who doesn't seem to be paying attention.

Briana smiles, clearly egged on by her friends' reactions. "Maybe she likes changing his diapers for him. She is a cleaning lady, after all." Her eyes swing toward me. "How about it, Rachel? Does your mom have you help her change Mr. Hammond's diapers?"

I can hear my pulse pounding in my ears. "Shut up," I say, but my voice is so soft, it's barely a whisper.

"Did you say something?" she says, coming closer. "Or were you just mouth-breathing again?"

I desperately want to stand up to Briana for once, but Caitlin's voice cuts in before I can say anything else: "Come on, Bree. We'll miss the bus."

Briana rolls her eyes. "God, Caitlin. Relax. We're going." She gives me a smirk before turning and striding away.

When I scan the lobby to find my mom, I spot Marisol standing nearby. For once, Angela isn't by her side. Based on the pitying look on Marisol's face, I can tell she saw the whole humiliating exchange.

I start to rush off in the other direction, but Marisol catches up with me.

"Here," she says, thrusting a paper bag into my hand with the words "Gray's Bakery and Catering" printed on the side.

"What's this?" I ask.

"Just open it."

For a second I wonder if this is Marisol's way of apologizing for our fight, but her mouth is pressed into a tight line that makes me suspect she still hasn't forgiven me for lying to her. Curiosity wins out, and I peek into the bag.

"A cookie?" I ask.

"A chocolate peanut-butter cookie," says Marisol. "Look familiar?"

It takes me less than a second to place it. "Angela's cookies from last year's bake sale."

Marisol nods. "She cheated. Her mom's friend owns Gray's Catering. They made the cookies, and Angela took the credit."

I stare down at the perfectly round pastry, remembering how crushed I was to lose to Angela. I was sure that my dessert would win. And now it turns out that Angela's victory was all a lie.

"Why are you telling me this?" I say. "I thought you and Angela were friends now."

"Because I know she's planning to cheat again. You should have won last year, and you deserve to win this time."

I close the paper bag and let it hang at my side. My

first instinct is to run over to Mr. Hammond and tell him all about Angela cheating. Maybe he'll even take away her cash prize from last year and give it to me.

But then I realize something: last year, my recipe almost beat Angela's, and her cookies were made by a *professional*. That means if I make my brownies perfect this year, maybe I can actually win, even if Angela cheats. If my recipe can beat a professional's, then I'll know I really am meant to be a pastry chef one day.

"So are you going to turn her in?" Marisol says.

"I won't need to. I'm going to beat Angela no matter what."

"But that's crazy. If you won't turn her in, then I will. It's not right for—"

"No," I say. "Just leave it alone. I don't need your help."

Marisol's face falls, and I instantly feel bad. I didn't mean to snap at her. I know she's just trying to help, but why can't she have more faith in me? She's always said how amazing my desserts are. Maybe she hasn't been that honest, after all.

"Fine," she says. "Suit yourself." Then, before I can tell her I'm sorry, she snatches the bag out of my hand and walks away.

● ● ●

For the rest of the week, I spend hours trying to find the perfect brownie recipe, but nothing works. I even manage to burn two batches of mint brownies, which makes the whole house smell like smoky toothpaste. Between the bake sale and the fact that I still don't have enough money to put back into my college fund, it feels like my whole life has turned into one big looming deadline. By Friday night, I'm starting to panic.

As I flip through my journal, I come to the latest entry in the Dirt Diary: details about what I found stashed in the Singh twins' closet. Apparently, they like to hide adult magazines behind their winter clothes. I almost screamed when I saw the magazines, and I couldn't stuff them back into their hiding place fast enough. That's the last time the twins' closet is getting a full cleaning, at least by me.

I'm about to shut the notebook when an idea zips through my head: I could use this information.

If I go to the twins and tell them what I found in their closet, who knows how much they'd pay me to keep quiet. Then I wouldn't have to stress about the bake-sale money. I'd have enough to put back in my bank account and maybe some extra to spare.

Holy candied apricots.

What is wrong with me? Am I really considering black-mailing a couple of seventh-graders? It's exactly what Marisol accused me of planning to do.

I shove the notebook away from me, wondering if I need to hide it behind *my* winter clothes. Just because I have all this dirt on people doesn't mean I should use it. No matter how desperate I am.

chapter 31

When we get to the Rileys' house on Saturday, I pray that Evan will be the one to open the door for us. I don't think I can handle dealing with Briana or Mrs. Riley. For once, my prayers are answered.

"Hey," he says, smiling at the sight of us. "Come on in."

"Thank you!" Mom chirps as we lug in our cleaning supplies. Evan quickly comes to help, and the three of us make our way into the kitchen. I can't help grinning at Evan as I remember our easy-flowing conversation outside of Marisol's house. He smiles back at me, which makes my stomach tingle like I've swallowed a handful of snowflakes.

"Rachel," Mom says, looking over the list Mrs. Riley left us. "We're supposed to wipe down some of the deck furniture. Do you mind cleaning in here while I go out and do that?" It's the most she's said to me in days.

"Sure." I have to admit I'm secretly glad that I get to stay inside with Evan.

After Mom goes through the sliding glass doors, Evan comes up beside me. "Do you want some help?" he asks.

It would be nice to have him do some of the work, but I'm the one getting paid. "Nah, that's okay. But you can keep me company if you want."

He smiles. "Absolutely."

It's amazing how relaxed I feel around Evan now. As I scrub and wipe, he follows me from room to room, and we chat about all kinds of things. He tells me about baseball and school and guitar lessons.

"I'm not all that good yet," he says, crunching on another peppermint candy. "But I'm hoping to start a band this summer."

I can just imagine how perfect he'd look on stage with a guitar. The image is so vivid in my head that it actually takes my breath away.

"Of course, my parents want me to spend less time playing and more time studying," he goes on.

"That sounds like my mom. She thinks cooking is a waste of time, even though it's what I want to do."

Evan nods. "My parents think there's no way I can be

an architect unless I have perfect grades. I guess I shouldn't complain. They're even harder on Briana."

"Really?"

He chuckles. "I know she can be a nightmare, but my parents have always pushed her really hard. She's naturally competitive, and they expect her to be perfect at everything she does. It kind of fuels the fire, you know?"

I think of the way Briana does everything to the extreme. I guess having parents who expect you to be the best at everything would be pretty rough. Not that it excuses how cruel Briana has been to me, but at least I understand her a little bit more. Until now, I pretty much thought of her as a movie villain.

"If they want her to be the best at everything, why doesn't she go to the same school as you?" I ask. Everyone knows Evan's academy is the best in the area.

Evan opens his mouth and then closes it again, like he isn't sure what to say.

"Wait," I say. "Don't tell me she didn't get in."

Evan's silence is all the answer I need. "Don't mention anything about it, okay?" he asks. "She's still pretty sensitive about the whole thing."

"Okay." I can't believe it. No wonder Evan is the only

person Briana listens to. He's the only one who's ever out-done her at anything.

I finish wiping the coffee table but stay put, not wanting our conversation to end. "So is that what you want to be, an architect?" I ask.

Evan shrugs. "Maybe. It's definitely something I'm interested in. But 'maybe' isn't good enough for my parents. They want me to have it all planned out now."

"Well, I think you're doing okay."

"Thanks." His green eyes sparkle at me like…green sparkles. Yup, I'm so caught up in them that I can barely think.

I want to keep talking to Evan, but I know Mom will come back inside soon, and I still have the bedrooms to do. Who knows what nightmare is waiting for me in Briana's room?

"Listen," I say, "I have to vacuum down here. But thanks for hanging out."

"Sure," he says. "Anytime." Then he heads upstairs, and I have to take deep breaths to keep my heart from pushing its way up into my throat. Why is he so nice to me? And why does he have to have a girlfriend? And since when do I go all gaga over a guy who isn't Steve Mueller?

I'm still in a weird dream state when I open the door to

Briana's room, but all my warm fuzzy feelings drain away as I realize the floor is covered with thumbtacks. All with their little points sticking up. All waiting for me to clean them up. Perfect.

chapter 32

Andrew is filming a zombie scene when I go up to his room. Since his parents aren't home and my mom went to meet with another possible cleaning client down the street, the house is silent. Somehow that makes Andrew's zombie figurines look even creepier.

He's so focused on his work that it takes him a good five minutes to notice me lurking in the hallway. Apparently "stop-motion animation" means moving the figurines about one millimeter, taking a picture, moving them another millimeter, and so on. I can't imagine anything more maddening, but Andrew seems totally in his element. I guess it's like me and baking.

"Rachel!" Andrew says, clearly surprised to see me standing in his doorway.

"Sorry, I didn't want to interrupt."

"How are the costumes coming along?"

I swallow. "Fine." In truth, I only managed to take the seams out of the Barbie clothes he gave me. I have yet to figure out how to put the fabric back together in a way that doesn't look awful.

"Will you have them done by next weekend?" he asks eagerly.

"Um, sure. I mean, I'll try."

"I really appreciate all your help, Rachel. It's so difficult doing this all on my own. I only hope—"

Bang!

Andrew and I both jump as something hits the window.

I whirl around and almost scream at the sight of blood oozing down the outside of the glass. Meanwhile, Andrew runs over to the window, throws it open, and yells: "I'm calling the police!"

I hurry over in time to see three boys zipping away on their bikes. I only recognize one of them, but I would know that spiky hair anywhere.

Steve Mueller.

I stare after the three figures until they disappear. What I thought was blood smells a lot like ketchup.

"I finally got them on film," Andrew says, smiling in triumph. "Now we can see who it is."

"It's Steve Mueller," I say, still feeling dazed.

Andrew looks at me. "Steve? Are you sure?"

I nod. "There were a couple others, but I only recognized him."

"Hopefully you can see all their faces on the video," he says, his cheeks flushed with excitement. "Then the police will have all the proof they need."

The police. How can Steve Mueller be involved with something like this? Even if he wasn't the one actually throwing things at Andrew's window, how could he stand by and let it happen? Maybe Marisol's right. Maybe I don't know Steve Mueller at all. Still, I can't let him get in trouble.

"Wait," I say. "Can you do me a favor and not go to the police yet?"

Andrew frowns. "Why?"

"I want to talk to Steve first. His friends must have put him up to it. I'm sure he didn't mean anything by it. Just give me a few days, okay? After that, you can do whatever you want with that video."

"All right," says Andrew with a shrug. "But you're wasting your time. Steve Mueller is just like the rest of them."

chapter 33

I expect Caitlin to be on the couch watching cooking shows again, but instead the house is eerily quiet when Ms. Montelle opens the door. I notice her eyes are red like she's been crying.

"Everything all right?" Mom asks, her voice soft and gentle.

Ms. Montelle nods, but she won't look at us. "If you don't mind, I'm just going to run out for a few minutes. Caitlin's in her room."

"Of course," Mom says. "Don't worry about a thing."

Ms. Montelle nods again. Then she grabs her car keys and rushes out the door.

"Poor woman," Mom says, clicking her tongue. She looks at me and lowers her voice to a whisper. "I don't know if you heard, but her ex-husband passed away a couple months ago."

I nod mutely. I've wanted to ask Mom about the

conversation I overheard, but I didn't want to admit to eavesdropping.

"They hadn't spoken in years," Mom goes on. "But that doesn't make things any easier." She glances down the hallway, toward Caitlin's room. "Anyway, I don't want to gossip. I just thought you should know since you and Caitlin are friends."

Wow. If Mom thinks Caitlin is my friend, she really has no clue about my life.

"Okay, I'll go start in the living room," she says. "Do you want to do the bedrooms?"

I can barely pick up the vacuum. Besides still feeling shaky from everything that happened at Andrew's house, my hands are throbbing from cleaning up all the thumbtacks in Briana's room. I was mostly able to scoop them up with a dustpan, but that didn't keep some from stabbing me.

When I go past Caitlin's room, I notice that her door is slightly ajar. I start to tiptoe past, hoping she won't pick that moment to come out. Then I freeze as I hear a horrible strangled sound, like something a hurt animal might make.

I'm pretty sure it came from Caitlin's room. A second later, it comes again, and I realize what it is. Caitlin's crying. Not just crying, sobbing.

I don't know what to do. Caitlin Schubert doesn't seem like someone who ever cries. And I'm probably the last person she wants to see. I consider going to get Mom, but then I think about how much worse her fix-it attitude always makes me feel when I'm upset. I can't inflict that on anyone, not even Caitlin.

The longer the crying goes on, the more I can't just stand there and pretend I don't hear it. Maybe I don't understand what she's going through, but I know how it feels to be sad and alone. I have to at least try to help. Maybe I've inherited some of Mom's fix-it-ness after all.

I put aside the vacuum and knock gently on the half-open door. Silence. Then another sob, softer this time.

Finally, I get up the courage to push the door open. "Hello?" I say, carefully peeking in. Caitlin is curled up on her bed, her arms wrapped around her knees. Her face is flushed like she's been crying for hours. She doesn't glance at me, just sits frozen like a statue, except for the tears still trickling down her face.

Behind her on the wall is a huge canvas that's splattered with angry colors. Glued to the canvas are bits of paper, ticket stubs, and even a wool glove. In the center of it all is a photo of a man's face. I know right away that he has to be Caitlin's father. He has her thin lips and dark, serious eyes.

"What are you doing here?" Caitlin mutters, pulling my attention away from the painting.

"Did you make that?" I ask.

She wipes her face with her hand. "Yeah. So?"

"It's amazing." Maybe it isn't the kind of art you'd see in a museum, but there's just so much genuine emotion in it. Way more than I've ever seen on Caitlin's perpetually sour face.

"It's just something I do when I'm..." She shakes her head and looks away.

"Um. Are you okay?" I finally manage, inching forward through piles of dirty clothes. It looks, and smells, like the room hasn't been cleaned in months.

Caitlin shifts so she's actually sort of facing me. "Why do you care?"

"I–I heard about your father. I'm really sorry."

Her eyes swing toward me. They're little slits that remind me of cat eyes. "Yeah, sure."

Okay, she's upset. But who is she to tell me whether or not I'm sorry? "I might not know what you're going through," I say. "But my parents just split up. I can't imagine what I'd do if I never saw my…" I can't even finish the sentence, the thought is so painful.

Caitlin stares at me for a minute, as if she thinks I might be making fun of her or something. Finally, she glances away. "I barely knew him. He would just send me money every month, like he was some distant relative or something. He said he wanted me to have all the best stuff, but he never came to visit. And then when he…died, his new wife got all his money. He didn't leave us anything."

I think of all the trips Caitlin and Briana have been on together, all their fancy clothes and shiny jewelry. That's how she could afford all those things. It also explains why Ms. Montelle has been working such long hours, why she looks so exhausted. She probably has to work twice as hard now that she isn't getting any help from her ex-husband.

Caitlin motions toward the canvas. "Those are the only things I have that were my dad's."

"That's nice," I say. "It's like a way to remember him."

"I guess. You know what the worst part is? I can't even talk to anyone about it. My mom thinks it's her fault somehow, and my friends…" She lets out a bitter laugh. "I don't even think I *have* friends anymore."

I want to laugh too. "Well, you're not alone there."

She looks at me. "What about that Parasol girl you're always hanging out with?"

"We had a fight." Feeling a little braver, I perch on the edge of Caitlin's bed, though I stay as far away from her as possible. "Is that what happened with you and Briana?"

Caitlin shakes her head. "No, it wasn't a fight. I don't know if Briana even realizes we're not friends anymore. All she cares about is softball and guys and herself." She wipes her eyes again. "You know what she said to me when I told her my dad died? She said I was lucky because now my mom would give me all kinds of pity presents to try to make it up to me. She actually wanted me to be happy about it!"

"Wow," I say, but really, after spending a half hour scooping thumbtacks off Briana's floor, it doesn't surprise me one bit.

"I guess when stuff like that happens, you find out who your actual friends are," Caitlin goes on. "I thought I could at least count on Steve, but even he's gotten different lately."

"Steve Mueller?" I think again of the ketchup on Andrew's window.

She nods, grabbing a tissue off her nightstand. "Our moms

have been friends forever, so we've known each other since we were born. We were even supposed to go on our first date a couple months ago, but then my mom got the call about my dad and I had to cancel. And before I knew it, Briana had snatched Steve up for herself. She didn't even like him before that. She just wanted him because she knew I liked him."

"Why would you even want to be friends with her?" I can't help asking.

"We used to have fun together when we were kids. I mean, Briana's always had a mean streak, but it didn't used to be so bad. But now…" She sighs and dabs at her red nose with the tissue. "Anyway, you don't have to sit here listening to me whine. I know you have work to do."

"Oh," I say, getting to my feet. "Well, good luck." It's a stupid thing to say, but it's the best I can do.

"Thanks," she says. "And, you know, thanks for listening. I guess you're not a total freak."

"Um, thanks."

I'm surprised to see her cheeks turn bright pink. "Sorry. I always say the wrong thing."

"You—you do?" I can't believe it. Caitlin always seems so sure of herself, like she's the smart one and everyone around her is dirt. Is she really as insecure as I am?

"Anyway. Thanks," she says.

I nod and leave her room. As I shut the door behind me, I'm still in shock that I just had something like a heart-to-heart with Caitlin Schubert. If I was wrong about her and about Steve, who else have I been wrong about?

chapter 34

On our way home that afternoon, Mom is singing along with the radio to a pop song I've always thought she hated. While I'm completely drained after such a long and crazy day, she seems like a cheerful ladybug. It's the happiest I've seen her since our fight.

"What's up, Mom?"

"Hmm?" she says, her mind clearly somewhere else.

"Why are you so happy all of a sudden?"

"Is that so unusual?"

"Um, yeah, these days it is." As good as she is at staying upbeat, I haven't seen Mom genuinely happy since Dad left. And, now that I think about it, long before that. She's always been so focused on making sure my dad and I were taken care of that she never laughed or had any actual fun.

"Well, I guess I had a good day, that's all."

"Does cleaning really put you in this good of a mood?" I ask.

Mom lets out a frustrated sigh. "All right, Rachel, if you must know, I'm happy because Robert called this morning and asked me out on a date."

I blink at her, sure I heard wrong. "Mr. Hammond...?"

"We're going out tomorrow. He's taking me to a museum and out to lunch."

My mind is swirling so fast that I don't know what to say first. What finally comes out is: "A museum? Since when do you like stuff like that?"

"I've always enjoyed art. I just haven't had much time to appreciate it."

"But you can't go on a date. Have you forgotten you're married? It's wrong!"

"No, it isn't wrong," says Mom. "Your father and I are officially separated now. The lawyer sent the paperwork the other day."

"What?" I practically shriek. "And when did you plan on telling me this?"

"You've haven't exactly been easy to talk to recently. I was waiting for the right time."

It feels like my lungs are about to burst. "So you're just going to replace Dad with Mr. Hammond?"

"Rachel, it's just a date!"

"You can't go out with him, Mom. He's old! He's like a geriatric patient."

She looks at me. "What are you talking about?"

"Haven't you noticed?" My face is burning from embarrassment, but I have to tell her. "The diapers? I saw them in his bathroom, tons of them. He's old, Mom. You can't go out with someone like that."

Mom's eyebrows shoot up. "So you're the one who's been spreading that terrible rumor around school?"

"What? No!"

"Rachel Lee, I know you have poor judgment sometimes, but how could you do something like that? The poor man has been through enough with his wife gone, and now you're telling everyone he wears diapers?"

"No! I—"

"For your information, those undergarments belong to his elderly mother. She stays with him during the winter. Not that you really deserve an explanation."

"But, Mom, it wasn't me. It was Marisol!"

Mom shakes her head, her lips a tight line. "Rachel, if you expect me to believe that Marisol would do something so childish, you really must think I'm a fool. She is not the kind of girl who would spread rumors."

Well, that shuts me right up. Because Mom is right. Marisol would never do that. It had to be someone else, someone who wanted to get in with the popular crowd. Someone like Angela Bareli.

"I promise, it wasn't me, okay?" I say. "Please trust me."

Mom sighs. "I do trust you, but the way you've been acting recently, I barely know you anymore. I understand you're upset about your father leaving us, but acting out isn't going to bring him back."

She pushes her hair away from her face, and that's when I notice it. The wedding band that's been on her finger for as long as I've been alive is gone.

"Rachel?" Mom says. "Are you listening to me?"

I blink. "What?"

"I said that I promise things will get easier. For now, I think we've been doing just fine without your father."

"Maybe you are, but I'm not!"

"Honey, I know you love him, but he's never been the most dependable person. I think it's time you realized that."

I turn away and stare out the window. It feels like someone just let all the air out of my body. If Mom is ready to move on, then maybe bringing Dad back won't make any difference anymore. Maybe it really is over.

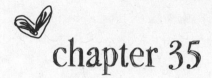

chapter 35

While Mom is out on her date the next day, I can't stop pacing around the house. I consider calling Marisol and telling her that I know she didn't spread the rumor about Mr. Hammond. But then again, she told Angela about the diapers after I swore her to secrecy, so she isn't totally blameless. Besides, I'm still ticked off at her, even though I really miss her.

I also know I have to call Dad and tell him I can't come down to Florida. Not only does it seem like Mom doesn't want him back, but there's no way I can save up enough money in the week I have left, and banking on the bake sale is crazy since I still haven't figured out a recipe. I'll have to pay fees and stuff to cancel the ticket, but at least I have enough cleaning money to cover those.

I go to pick up the phone to call Dad but don't actually dial his number. I just can't imagine telling him the truth.

So instead I decide to make some cream puffs since I'm completely sick of brownies. It won't get me any closer to figuring out my problems, but maybe it'll make me feel better.

As I'm getting the ingredients together, my phone rings. My pulse gets all fluttery when I see it's Dad calling. He must have psychically known that I need to talk to him.

"What are you up to, Roo?" he asks.

"Just making some cream puffs," I say, trying to keep my voice steady.

He whistles. "You bake fancier things every time I talk to you."

"They're actually not that hard to make." I start explaining the process, but Dad just laughs.

"You know I'm useless in the kitchen, Roo. What you're saying is pure gibberish to me. You'll just have to make me some of those cream puffs when you come down here."

"About that…" I take a deep breath, knowing I have to tell him the truth. If I can explain things and have him on my side, he might be able to convince Mom to go easy on me. "Dad, I have to—"

"There's something I want to tell you," he says over my tiny whisper. "You're going to find out for yourself when you come down here, so I guess I should just fill you in now."

"What is it?"

"Well, honey. The thing is…that I met someone down here. She's a very sweet lady, and I think you'll like her a lot."

Wait, what? He what? *What?*

"I know this is a bit of a surprise," Dad goes on. "It wasn't anything I planned, but life is funny like that sometimes. Now I don't want you to be upset. And please don't mention anything to your mom, at least not yet. I want to be the one to tell her. Will you let me do that?"

I try to breathe.

"Roo?"

It's over. All over. If my mom is on a date and my dad met someone else, then our family is really gone. "So you're not coming back," I whisper.

"I'm sorry, Roo. Not this time."

It takes me a second to understand what he said. "What do you mean, 'this time'?"

He lets out a long sigh. "I guess you were too young to remember, but your mother and I took a break a few years back. You must have been in kindergarten."

"What are you talking about?" I might not remember much from when I was five, but wouldn't I remember my parents splitting up?

"After a few weeks, your mother and I decided to give it another shot. For your sake. But it's just not going to work this time."

He keeps talking, but I'm not listening anymore. I can't believe it. No wonder Mom has been so determined to move on with her life. No wonder she keeps telling me my father can't be trusted.

I realize Dad is saying my name over and over. "Rachel, are you still there?"

The room is swaying around me. "Why didn't you tell me you'd left before?"

"It was only for a month," he says. "You were so young that you barely knew what was going on. We hoped you'd just forget."

I had forgotten, but maybe part of me hadn't. Maybe that's why I was so afraid of doing or saying the wrong thing all the time. Maybe I'd thought my dad leaving had something to do with me.

"Who—who is she?" I ask, trying to keep the tears back. Because once they start, they might never stop. "What's her name?"

"Her name is Ellie. She was one of my first scuba clients."

"Did you move there for her?"

"No! I only met her after I was down here. Trust me, Roo, I never…"

I stop listening, not wanting to hear anything else he has to say. How can he think I'll be all right with him finding someone else? He left us behind and is going to start a life with someone new. And here I was stupidly thinking that I could fly down to visit him and patch everything up. As if one little trip could make any difference. Marisol was right.

"Roo? Are you still there?"

"I'm not coming to visit."

"What? Why not?"

"Why not?" I repeat, my voice shrill to my own ears. "Are you serious? You can't just leave me and think I'll be fine with it. You can't just dump Mom and start seeing someone else and think I'll be fine with it. You can't—"

"That's not what I did, and you know it, Roo. I thought you were mature enough that I could be honest with you. But I guess I was wrong."

"*I'm* the one who's immature?" I yell. "You're the one who abandoned your family to go start a business you don't know anything about!"

"Rachel—"

"I've been going crazy trying to save up the money to come see you, and now it's all for nothing!"

"Rachel—"

"I don't want to hear anything you have to say, Dad. Mom was right. We're better off without you."

Before he can say another word, I hang up and slam my cell phone down on the counter. It skids off the edge and lands on the floor with a dull thud. I probably just broke my phone, but I don't even care.

I leave the half-made cream puffs on the counter, run to my room, and throw myself on my bed. I've never been so furious with my dad in my entire life. Before I met Marisol, Dad was always the one I went to when I was upset, but this time there's no one to talk to.

The tears threaten to burst out of me, but I squeeze my pillow until my eyes stop burning. Dad isn't worth crying over, not anymore. I did enough of that when he left.

It was stupid of me to think I could fix things, but it turns out Mom has the right idea. It's time to think ahead and not focus on the things we can't change.

With that thought bouncing around in my head, I go back out to the kitchen and put the cream puffs in the oven. Then I do something totally crazy, as if an alien has possessed my body. I grab my phone off the floor (luckily it still works) and dial the Rileys' number.

"Hello?" Briana's voice says.

I almost hang up right there, but that strange alien force is still controlling me. "Hi, is Evan there?"

"Yeah, hold on." And that's it. No ridicule. No insults. She had no idea it was me. Maybe Briana Riley doesn't have a humiliation superpower after all.

"Hello?" says Evan.

"Hey, it's Rachel," I say, my voice quivering a little bit.

"Oh, hi. How are you?"

"Not great," I say. "I have a ton of cream puffs and no one to eat them with. And there's an episode of *Pastry Wars* starting in an hour, and I have no one to watch it with."

"Wow, that's quite the pickle you're in." I can hear the smile in his voice. "I guess the least I can do is come over and help you out. I just need your address."

As I give him directions to my house, the reality of what I'm doing hits me like a frying pan to the face. Oh my goldfish. I just invited a guy over to hang out with me. And I did it without having a complete giggling fit or a loss of bodily functions. And he actually said yes! Okay, so he has a girlfriend. It's not a date. But that doesn't matter. I just need a friend, and it turns out Evan actually falls into that category.

chapter 36

When Evan rings the doorbell, I nearly have a heart attack. I've never had a guy over to my house, not even to work on a school project or anything. In fact, I have no idea how my mom would feel about me having a boy over. But I decide not to worry about that right now.

"Hi," I say after I open the door. My cheeks hurt from the crazy grin on my face. Calm down, I tell myself. You don't want to scare him off.

"Hey," says Evan. "Are you going to let me in?"

"Oh." I realize I'm just standing in the doorway, staring at him. I let him inside and lead him into the kitchen. I must have been channeling my mom because I've spent the past half hour furiously cleaning the house in preparation for Evan's visit, even though it was already pretty spotless.

"Those cream puffs look amazing," Evan says. He turns

back to me, and that's when he must notice the misery I'm trying to hide. "Are you okay?"

I mean to lie and tell him that I'm fine, but I find myself saying, "My dad met another woman. He's not coming back."

"Wow, I'm really sorry. Do you want to talk about it?"

I'm surprised to discover that I don't, not at all. I said all I had to say to my dad. "Actually, I kind of just want to watch TV and get my mind off things."

"Fair enough," says Evan.

But as we start to watch the show, I have a hard time keeping my mind on the elaborate pastries. All I can think about is what Dad said about leaving when I was a kid. That's why Mom tried so hard to move on, because she'd been through it before, and this time she knew he'd left for good.

"Rachel, are you okay?" Evan asks.

I snap back to reality and realize the credits of *Pastry Wars* are rolling and that I missed pretty much the whole show.

"No. I mean yeah. I guess I'm just distracted." And then I find myself telling him all about the phone conversation I had with my dad. "Sorry," I say when I'm done. "I shouldn't have invited you over when I'm such a mess."

Evan looks at me. "I don't think you're a mess. In fact, I think you're pretty awesome."

My face goes boiling hot, but for once it isn't from being mortified. I can't stop grinning as we go back to watching TV. As angry as I am about everything that my dad has put my family through, I'm glad that at least something good has come of it all.

But as much as I want to enjoy hanging out with Evan, I keep thinking about the plane ticket and the money and everything else that's happened in the past few weeks.

I get to my feet. "Hold on, I have to go take care of something. I'll be back in a minute." I have to cancel that plane ticket now, before I'm tempted to change my mind.

But just as I sit down at my computer, I hear Mom come through the front door.

"Ray-chul, where are you?" she calls in a voice that tells me I'm in huge trouble. Uh-oh. Poor unsuspecting Evan is in the living room all by himself.

I rush out to rescue him, even though I'm dreading whatever it is Mom's going to yell at me about. When I get there, I see she's holding a piece of paper with a bank logo on it. Oh no. She knows. She knows everything.

I can practically hear a buzzer go off in my head. Time's up. Game over.

"Rachel," Mom says, her voice a scary kind of calm. "Can you ask your guest to leave, please?"

Evan shoots to his feet, looking ready to run.

"Thanks for coming over," I tell him, hoping the "I am so incredibly sorry" is implied.

He gives me a weak smile and darts for the door. Then I'm left all alone with Mom. I expect her to start yelling, but instead she goes over to the couch and sinks into it with a heavy sigh.

"Come sit down," she orders.

I obey, trying not to get too close in case she starts shooting fireballs out of her eyes.

"Do you know what the first thing I did was after you were born?" she says. "I went to the bank and opened a savings account in your name. I'd spent years working one terrible job after another, each boss more clueless than the next, and I never wanted you to have to do that." She looks over at me, her eyes hard. "But the thing about that money, Rachel, is that even though it's for your college education, it isn't your money. It's *my* money. And I decide how it's spent, do you understand?"

I nod, knowing it's pointless to argue.

"But you didn't understand that a few weeks ago, because if you had, you wouldn't have withdrawn three hundred dollars! Am I right?"

I realize she wants an actual answer. "You're right," I whisper.

"So what did you do with that money, Rachel? What did you need it for?"

I don't want to admit how stupid I was in thinking I could get Dad to come back to us, but I have to tell her something. Mom is too mad to just let it go without an explanation.

"Was it for a dress?" she says. "Is that what was so important that you couldn't ask me first?"

I gawk at her. "A dress? Do you really think I'd take money out for something like that?"

"Well, you seemed excited to be going to the Spring Dance. And since you don't talk to me about anything, that's all I had to go on."

"This is exactly why I don't talk to you about stuff!" I say. "Because you take what I say and totally twist it around."

"Stop trying to change the subject. If the money wasn't for a dress, then what did you need it for?"

I look away.

"Rachel, tell me this second!" she demands.

"Fine." I hug a throw pillow to my chest like it's armor. Time to come clean. "It was for a plane ticket."

Mom's eyes practically fall out of her head. "A plane ticket?"

"I know it was stupid, okay? But I thought that if I could just go down to Florida and see Dad, he might remember how much he missed us, and then he'd change his mind and come home. I was going to pay back the money as soon as I could. I didn't want to use it at all, but I didn't have any choice."

"So you were just going to fly down to Florida without telling me?"

"No, I was going to wait until I had the money and then I was going to tell you. I wasn't planning to run away or anything. I just knew you wouldn't understand."

"You're right. I don't understand how you could do something like this behind my back. If you really wanted to go down to visit your father, we could have talked about it."

"We did talk about it, remember? And you said no. You said I needed to learn to live without Dad. You'd already given up on him, on getting our family back together. But I couldn't sit by and do nothing!"

Mom closes her eyes for a second. "I hadn't given up, Rachel. I just knew there was nothing left to fight for. And I didn't want you to go to Florida and come home heartbroken."

I think of the way Dad accused me of being immature when I got upset about his new girlfriend. I guess Mom's right. If I'd gone down to Florida, things wouldn't have gotten better. Maybe I would have been even more crushed than I am now.

"So," Mom says, turning to me. "You're going to return that ticket and put back that money. If you can save up for the trip on your own, then we'll talk about it. But you're not going to jeopardize your future to go traipsing down to Florida to try to talk sense into your father."

"I'm not going, okay? You were right. It was stupid of me to think it could work. Besides, Dad is the last person I want to see right now. I'm going to return the ticket today."

"Good," says Mom. Then she frowns. "What do you mean, your father is the last person you want to see?"

"Nothing."

"What happened? Tell me."

Even though Dad told me not to tell Mom, I don't have a choice. Because she deserves to know the truth, and I

can't hold the secret in for a minute longer. "He met someone else! He's never coming back to us now."

Mom sits back, looking like she's just been slapped
across the face. "He met someone else," she repeats.

"He doesn't care that we miss him," I say. "All he cares
about is himself. You were right. He didn't want us there
with him. And he told me about last time, about how he
left when I was a kid."

Mom nods slowly, like I just answered a silent question
in her head. She looks over at me and seems surprised to
find that I'm crying. "Come here," she says, patting the
spot beside her.

I slide toward her, expecting her to yell at me some
more, to rub it in my face that she was right about my dad.
But instead, she reaches out and wraps her arms around
me. "Your father loves you, Rachel. And I do too. You
never have to doubt that, okay?"

"Okay," I say. And even though hearing that doesn't
make everything right again, having my mom just be my
mom, instead of Ms. Fix-It, makes me feel a little better.
"Why didn't you tell me that he'd left before?"

Mom sighs. "I thought about telling you, but the truth
is, I didn't want to remember. It was such a hard time for

us. Your father ran off to Texas to work on a cattle ranch, and I thought he'd lost his mind. After a few weeks, he came back and promised he'd never do anything like that again. And for a while, things were really good. I convinced myself that his running away hadn't meant anything."

"Why didn't you tell me about it when he left this time? Then maybe I wouldn't have kept hoping he'd come back."

My mom looks at me with tears in her eyes. "You're right. I should have. I thought I was protecting you, but I guess I only made things worse for you." She starts crying so hard that it makes her entire body shake.

"It's okay," I tell her, putting my arms around her shoulders. "It's not your fault." And I realize as I say it that it's true. Mom's always tried to fix everything, but there's no way she could have fixed Dad leaving. She wasn't able to do it then, and she can't do it now. Neither one of us can.

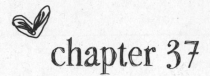

chapter 37

I expect Mom to sentence me to a year's worth of embarrassing labor, but I guess she feels bad for me since she only grounds me for the rest of the school year. Unfortunately, that includes the Spring Dance. I feel like a jerk having to tell Andrew that I can't go with him, but I decide to put it off for now. Maybe I can find a way to get out of my grounding and go to the dance after all.

When I see Caitlin in homeroom on Monday, she looks a little less miserable than she has the past few weeks. As Briana babbles on about softball, Caitlin glances over at me, and I dare to give her a tiny smile. She looks right through me before turning back to give Briana her full attention.

My stomach dips. Of course Caitlin won't acknowledge me in school, especially not in front of Briana. She probably only spilled her guts to me on Saturday because she was too upset to care who she was talking to. It was stupid to think Caitlin Schubert and I had anything in common.

I spend the rest of the morning in total gloom. When I go to the Home Ec room during lunch, I just sit there with the apron on my lap. For the first time in my life, I don't feel like baking anything. I still have no idea what I'm going to make for the bake sale next Monday, and I'm starting to wonder if there's any point in competing. Let Angela Bareli cheat her way to winning again. It isn't going to bring my family back together or make Marisol forgive me.

Ms. Kennedy doesn't ask what's wrong, but she hands me a chocolate chip cookie and says, "You know I'm here if you need anything."

"Thanks," I say. But the problem is, I don't even know what I need. There isn't any way to make my life go back to normal, not after everything that's happened. And even Ms. Kennedy's sympathetic smile isn't comforting. In fact, it actually makes me feel worse.

I put aside the untouched cookie and rush out of the room. Even though I've never skipped class in my life, part of me wants to run out of the school and just keep going. Maybe then my heart will stop aching.

As I swing around the corner, I catch sight of someone at my locker. As I get closer, I realize the person is Briana, and she has something in her hands.

Oh, holy baked haddock. It's the Dirt Diary. She has the diary, and she's reading it.

"What are you doing?" I say.

She looks up, not even surprised, and smiles. "Rachel Lee," she says. "You sure write some interesting things."

"Give it back." My mind is swirling. Did I write anything about my deal with Steve in the diary? No. At least that secret is safe.

"Sure." She snaps the notebook shut and slips it back into my locker. "I read it all the way through already. Wait until I tell everyone what you've been saying about them." She laughs. "I bet Steve will love to hear how you've been drooling over him. And Evan too."

I feel my cheeks ignite. "You had no right to read that. It's mine."

She shrugs. "It's not my fault your locker was just standing open when I walked by."

Of course, it *is* her fault. If she hadn't glued it shut, the janitor wouldn't have had to pry it open, and then my locker would actually lock like it's supposed to.

"Why can't you just leave me alone?" I say. "Why do you have to keep doing this stuff to me?"

She shrugs. "Because it's too much fun."

I stare at her, totally helpless. She'll tell everyone about the things in my notebook, and everyone will hate me more than they already do. And, worst of all, Evan will think I'm some kind of stalker. I want to scream at her or shake her until her earrings fall out, but none of it will do any good. My pathetic excuse for a life is over.

Suddenly, another voice echoes down the hall: "Hey, Briana."

I turn to find Caitlin standing behind me. There's a spark in her eyes for the first time in weeks.

Briana lets out an impatient sigh. "There you are. I thought you'd ditched me."

"I wish I had," says Caitlin. "Years ago. Then I wouldn't have to stand by and watch you pull off all your stupid pranks."

Briana rolls her eyes. "You didn't seem to care when I glued Rachel's locker shut."

"I figured one time couldn't hurt," says Caitlin. "But it's getting old."

"What happened to you?" Briana says. "You used to be

fun. Now you're like this moody lump all the time. I know there was all that stuff with your father, but you have to get over it sometime, don't you?"

Caitlin shrugs. "I guess I finally figured out who my friends are."

"What's that supposed to mean? Are you going to be friends with freaks like Rachel Lee from now on?"

Caitlin folds her arms in front of her chest. She looks almost like her old self again. "It means that you either stop messing with people or I tell everyone about your bras."

Briana gasps, her eyes widening. "You wouldn't do that."

"Yes, I would," says Caitlin. "If you breathe a word of what's in Rachel's notebook, I'll make sure your secret gets all around school."

The two of them stare each other down for a long moment, like some silent battle of wills. Then Caitlin gives me a little smile, whirls around, and stomps down the hall.

Instantly, Briana rushes past me. "Caitlin, wait!" she calls. "You're right. I'm sorry." Then both their footsteps fade away.

I stand there with my jaw practically on the floor. I can't believe Caitlin Schubert actually stood up for me. I don't know what she meant about Briana's bras, but that doesn't matter. All I care about is that Caitlin has a piece of dirt on Briana that's so bad, I won't have to worry about her torturing me again. Maybe Caitlin Schubert and I will never be friend material, but right now she feels like my best friend in the whole world.

chapter 38

Steve Mueller comes to my locker the next day, his face unusually serious. For the first time in over a year, I don't have that familiar bubbly feeling in my stomach at the sight of him. All I can think about is how he's been bullying Andrew.

"So I found another note last night," he says.

"Note?"

He leans in and his cologne shoots up my nostrils. "Yeah, in Briana's room. I went through her desk when she was in the bathroom. This one was signed."

Oh my goldfish. The fake secret admirer I invented is *real*? "Who was it from?"

"Some guy named Kurt. Do you know him?"

I shake my head before realizing that I *do* know someone named Kurt. Is it possible Briana's cheating with Evan's teammate? Remembering Kurt's hot breath on my face, his mocking tone, makes me shudder. He and Briana deserve each other.

"I need you to go look through her room for me one more time," says Steve.

"Sorry, I don't think so." My days of snooping are over. From now on, I'm going to earn my money the honest way, one smelly toilet at a time.

"Please," says Steve. "If I break up with her and then it turns out the note was old or something, it'll all be for nothing."

"Why don't you just ask her about it?" Pretty ironic, me telling someone else to talk something out, but still.

He shakes his head. "Briana's really sensitive. If I say anything, she'll think I'm accusing her and flip out."

Nice girlfriend. "Are you sure you really want to be dating her?" I can't help asking.

Steve looks surprised at my question. For some reason, that gives me the courage to keep talking.

"Okay, here's the deal," I say. "I'll take one more look around Briana's room. I'll even do it for free. But only if you promise to leave Andrew Ivanoff alone. No more vandalizing his house. Got it?"

Steve shrugs. "It's not like we hurt anyone. It was just—"

"A joke? Well, it wasn't funny. I don't know what

happened to you. Ever since you started dating Briana, you've been acting like a jerk."

His eyes widen. "Say what?"

"I used to think you were this super nice guy, and I'd defend you when people said you were just like all the other popular kids. But I think I was wrong." I can't believe I'm saying this to Steve Mueller. *The* Steve Mueller! But I can't keep it inside a minute longer.

"I *am* a nice guy," he insists.

"Oh really? Would a nice guy throw fake blood at someone's window and ask me to snoop around his girl-friend's room?"

Steve's dimpled cheeks get red. "You don't understand—"

"And I'm not the only who's noticed how much you've changed. Caitlin thinks so too."

"She said that?" Steve seems to think this over for a minute. Finally, he nods. "I promise, if you look around Briana's room one more time, that'll be the end of it. I won't ask you to do it anymore. I just need to know the truth. And don't worry about Andrew. We'll leave him alone from now on." He looks down at me, and there's something like amusement in his eyes. "I always thought you were really quiet. I never realized you had so much to say."

I almost laugh. "I guess I didn't either."

As I watch him walk away, I expect to be disappointed not to have those gooey feelings about Steve anymore. But I'm actually relieved. Okay, it was fun to obsess over him for the past year, but now I know for sure that nothing will ever happen between us, and I'm okay with that. In fact, I'm not even sure I'd want to date someone like Steve Mueller. Like Marisol said, there has to be someone much better out there for me.

chapter 39

As Mom and I unload the minivan outside the Rileys' house on Saturday morning, I notice the "mop" label on our mop has disappeared. As much as I hate to admit it, I know I have Mr. Hammond to thank for my mom's returning sanity. Because of his easygoing personality, she's started taking things a little less seriously. I wonder if his influence will mean my grounding will be cut short so I can go to the Spring Dance after all, but that's probably too much to hope for.

When I open the door to Briana's room, I expect to find new horrors staring back at me. But everything looks normal. Then I take a step forward, and something crunches under my feet. Oh my goldfish. The entire carpet has been sprinkled with glass.

This is a new low, even for Briana. I guess this is her way of getting back at me after what happened with Caitlin.

Pulling off her worst prank yet as some kind of last hurrah. There's no way to clean up all the glass, not without cutting myself a million times in the process.

Still, I have no choice but to at least try. But first, I want to get the snooping over with. Then I'll deal with the impossible glass problem.

I crunch over to Briana's desk and look through it one more time. I don't know where Steve found the note, but I don't see anything else. Then I notice that the door to the walk-in closet is open. Ever since that first day when Briana found me going through her things, she's kept her closet tightly shut. Maybe she's hiding something in there?

I go inside the closet and look around for anything that could be a hiding spot. After a minute, my eyes fall on the rows of Briana's bras, and I remember what Caitlin said to her in the hallway.

As I get closer, I notice that even Briana's sports bras are hung up, which is beyond weird. When I hold up one of the lacy bras, I realize it doesn't have regular padding. Instead, the bra is heavy and stiff, and the fabric is much firmer than foam. When I inspect the sports bras, I find the same kind of padding sewn into them.

It takes me a minute to believe what I'm seeing, but

there's no other explanation. Briana Riley stuffs her bra! Of course, she does it in the rich-kid way: she has bras specially made for her so that no one will suspect. Ever since the first day of sixth grade, all the girls have been jealous of Briana's perfect chest and the attention it gets from guys. And all this time, it's been a fake. No wonder Briana was so ready to apologize when Caitlin threatened to expose her secret.

How's that for an entry in the Dirt Diary?

What'll happen if everyone at school finds out the truth? My mind swirls with the possibilities. But then I realize I can't tell anyone, because if I do, then I'll be just as bad as Briana or Angela. And if there's one thing I've learned, it's that secrets make me feel like scum.

I put the bra back where I found it and go back to searching. I finally give up on the closet, and my eyes fall on the TV stand in the corner. In my rush last time, I didn't check there.

There's nothing behind the TV, but when I open a drawer that's supposed to be for movies, there's a jewelry box staring back at me. I carefully lift it out and open it. There are only a few things inside. A silver heart necklace, a matching bracelet, and a couple of greeting cards. I open one of the cards and hit the jackpot. It's a note from Kurt, telling Briana how special she is and how he hopes she'll finally dump Steve for him.

I'm just deciding whether or not to pocket the note to show Steve when I hear someone clear his throat behind me.

I jump up and see Evan standing in the doorway.

"Evan, hi," I say, still holding the jewelry box. I can't imagine how guilty I must look.

"What are you doing?" he says, unsmiling.

"Um. Well, it's kind of a long story. But it's not what it looks like, not really."

"What it looks like is that you're going through my sister's stuff. Is that not what you're doing?"

"Er. Okay, kind of. But it's for a good reason." My body suddenly feels hot and jittery, like I've just sprinted a mile. "You see, her boyfriend was afraid she was cheating on him, so he paid me to look around her room."

"He *paid* you?"

"Well, at first. But then I said I'd do it for free." Oh no. This is sounding worse and worse. "I'm not doing a very good job of explaining, but—"

"I came in here once, and it looked like you were going through Briana's drawers, but I told myself that I was just being paranoid. I mean, why would you be doing that? But here you are again. And now I find out you've been doing it for a while."

The jitteriness is so bad now that my teeth are actually chattering. "Evan, I'm sorry. It was just—"

"I think you should be apologizing to Briana, not me." He shakes his head. "I don't get it. I mean, I was really starting to like you. I was even jealous that someone else had asked you to the dance."

I take a step back, and the carpet crunches under my foot. The jitters fade, replaced by a strange warm feeling in the pit of my stomach. "You were?" I say. "But I thought you had a girlfriend."

He frowns. "I don't have a girlfriend. Who told you that?"

"Well, I saw that picture on your computer—"

"You were on my computer?"

"No!" Why is it that no matter what I say, it just sounds bad?

"The girl in the picture is my cousin. She goes to my school," says Evan. Then he shakes his head, like he can't make sense of what's happening. "Briana warned me that first day. She said you couldn't be trusted. I didn't want to believe her, but now I don't know what to think."

"Evan, I'm really sorry. I swear, I can explain."

He won't look at me. "I think you should probably just go."

"But—"

"Please, Rachel."

It's no use. He hates me. I want to cry, but instead I shove the jewelry box back in its hiding place and close the drawer. Then I crunch my way toward the door.

"Is that *glass* on the floor?" Evan asks.

"Don't worry, I'll clean it up."

But suddenly Mom is in the doorway. "No, you won't. That's ridiculous. You can't be expected to clean up something like that! It's unsafe." She turns to Evan. "Tell your mother that we're very sorry, but that she'll have to get someone else to take care of this mess. Come on, Rachel."

Mom takes my hand, and I'm glad to let her lead me downstairs. I don't even bother looking back.

As we pack up the car, my head is ringing like a giant bell. "Are we going to lose this job?" I ask.

Mom shrugs. "Maybe. But I am sick of Mrs. Riley's attitude. And if they expect us to clean up hazardous materials, then I say good riddance. I think you were right about us taking this job, honey. It was a bad idea from the start."

"But what about the other jobs? If Mrs. Riley spreads the word, won't other people fire us?"

"I was worried about that at first, but Ms. Montelle is a well-respected woman in this town, and she happens to be a big fan of ours. I think we'll be fine. And if people do give us a hard time, we'll just travel a little farther for work. There are dirty houses everywhere." She smiles, and I can't help feeling relieved. At least that's one less thing to worry about. Because thinking about how betrayed Evan looked is about all the pain I can handle.

chapter 40

When it's time for our usual lunch break, I expect Mom to grab some sandwiches from a cooler so we can eat them in the car. Not that I'm hungry. Everything that happened with Evan has filled my stomach with rocks.

Instead, Mom drives into town and pulls up in front of Molly's Diner.

"What are we doing?" I ask.

"I think we could both use a treat," she says, opening the car door.

As I stare out the window at the cheerful Molly's sign, my body refuses to move.

"What's the matter?" Mom asks, realizing I'm not following her.

"I don't want to go in there. That was our place, when we were still a family. It doesn't feel right anymore."

"I know things are different." Mom leans back in her

seat. "But does that mean we can't do any of the old things anymore?"

"I don't know," I admit. "It just feels wrong to come here without Dad."

Mom puts her hand on top of mine. It feels warm and reassuring. I realize this is the most honest I've been with her in forever, besides the times when I've lost it and screamed at her.

"How about we give it a try?" she says. "If it's terrible, we'll leave and go somewhere else. I promise."

That sounds reasonable, even if I'm still not thrilled about it. Besides, Mom is clearly making an effort to make me feel better, even after I lied to her and went behind her back. I owe it to her to at least try.

When we go inside, the familiar smells of coffee and maple syrup hit me like a slap. I have to swallow the tears that threaten to leak down my cheeks. I'm about to tell Mom that I can't do this, that we have to go, when she wraps her fingers around mine. Suddenly, I feel like a little kid again, safe and warm.

Before I know it, we're seated at a tiny table in the corner, far from our usual spot, and Mom is ordering two hot chocolates.

"Are you okay?" she asks after the waitress goes to get our drinks.

I nod, realizing that, surprisingly, I *am* okay. It still feels strange to be here without Dad, but Molly's has been my favorite place for as long as I can remember. Being here brings a little bit of comfort with it, even if it also brings up painful memories.

"Now, what are we going to order?" Mom asks, grabbing a menu.

I have to laugh. "We've only been getting the exact same thing for like ten years."

She smiles and pushes the menu away. "Good. Now that that's decided, we'll have more time to talk."

"Talk?" I say, thinking of all the awkward dinner conversations we've had since Dad left.

"I know you and your father were always close," she says. "And I have to tell you that I've always been a little jealous of that. I always wished that we were able to open up to each other the way you and your father could. Now that it's just you and me, I want us to find a way to talk to one another."

I blink. Never in a million years did I think my mom was jealous of my relationship with my dad. She's always seemed too uptight to join in our silly games and our bad jokes. But now that I think about it, maybe she was just always too stressed out trying to keep our family together to be able to loosen up.

"Me too," I say.

"Okay, then talk to me," says Mom. "I know you've been miserable this year. I could tell something was wrong even before your father left. What's been going on?"

My instinct is to shrug it off and tell her it's nothing, but the truth is, I want to find a way to make her understand what I've been going through. "First, you have to promise me you won't try to fix anything."

"Fix anything?" she repeats. "What do you mean?"

"It's my problem, and I'll find a solution, okay?"

Mom takes in a deep breath and then nods. "Okay."

So I start telling her about everything that's happened since the start of the year, about Fake Boyfriend Troy, about Briana and Caitlin, and even about Steve Mueller. Before I know it, I'm even telling her about Evan Riley! I have to look down at my napkin as my cheeks burn with embarrassment, but I don't hold anything back. The only thing I don't mention is the Dirt Diary. It feels wrong to talk about secrets that aren't mine.

When I'm done talking, I glance up expecting to find Mom judging everything I just told her, but instead she's smiling gently, her eyes glistening.

"Thank you for trusting me," she says. "And if there's anything you need, any way that I can help, just tell me, okay? That's what I'm here for."

I nod, knowing that she means it. It's up to me to fix all the things I messed up, but it's still nice that Mom genuinely wants to help. Not because she's dying to butt in and take over my life, but because she really wants me to be happy.

The waitress comes back with our orders, which gives Mom a chance to wipe her eyes. As I glance down at my Nutella and banana crepe, my stomach rumbles so loudly that even my mom hears it across the table.

She laughs as she bites into her own crepe, which is filled with apples and brie.

"You know," I say as I dig into my food. "There is one thing you could help me with. The bake sale is this Monday, and I still haven't figured out what to make."

"What have you tried so far?" she asks.

I go through all the different kinds of brownies I've baked, none of which have been good enough.

"Hmm," Mom says, chewing thoughtfully. "It sounds like you were pretty unhappy when you came up with those recipes. Maybe you should try to make something when you're feeling more positive."

My first instinct is to brush off what she said as more of her power-of-determination advice. But I realize she's right. I made coconut brownies when I desperately missed Dad, cayenne pepper brownies when I was furious, and sea-salt brownies when I was upset. But I never tried making anything when I was happy. Probably because I haven't been much of that lately.

My mouth drops open, making a piece of crepe fall out onto the table. "Mom, you're a genius!" I can't believe the answer has been staring me right in the face all this time, and I didn't see it. But now I have it, and it's perfect. There is no way I'm going to lose to Angela or to anyone else this time.

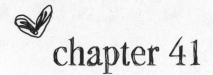

chapter 41

My good mood evaporates as we pull up to the Ivanoffs' house later that day. I'd been hoping that if I could make amazing costumes for the dolls in Andrew's movie, then I'd have an easier time breaking the news about not being able to go to the dance with him. But what I've actually made are asymmetrical capes that look like they were sewn by someone without opposable thumbs. Andrew is going to hate me on so many levels.

After Mom and I finish cleaning the Ivanoffs' house, she insists on going ahead to the next house without me so I can talk to Andrew. "Take all the time you need," she says, squeezing my arm.

I nod and promise to call her when I'm done. Then I take a deep breath before heading up the stairs to Andrew's room, the bag of terrible capes in tow.

When I show him the costumes, Andrew tries to act like

they're not the ugliest things in the world. But unless he's been drinking glue, he can see just how awful they are.

"I'm so sorry," I tell him. "I'll redo them. The next ones will be a lot better."

"I'm sort of running out of time," he says. "I have to finish shooting in the next few days. But if you think you'll be able to do them soon…" He glances down at the pile of hideous Barbie capes and nervously runs his hand over his pale hair.

The capes took me forever to make. There's no way I can crank out new, better outfits in only a couple days.

I feel horrible. Andrew trusted me, which wasn't easy for him considering that he seems terrified of all humans, and I let him down. If I'd just sent Marisol his way from the beginning, it would've been okay. But I can't go running to Marisol now, can I? What if I try to apologize to her and she shoots me down?

Then again, can I really live with myself if Andrew doesn't get into film camp because of how terrible I made his movie look? No, I have to suck up my pride and ask Marisol for help. Even if it means making a total fool out of myself.

"I'll fix this," I tell Andrew. "Don't worry."

"Okay," he says, not looking convinced. "Were you able to talk to Steve Mueller?"

"Yeah, and he promised that he and his friends would leave you alone from now on. Are you still going to take that video to the police?"

Andrew shrugs. "I'm not sure. I don't want to just let it go. People should pay for their mistakes."

I think of all the mistakes I've made, especially in the past few weeks. How long will I be paying for all those bad decisions?

"But," Andrew goes on, "if it really won't happen again, then I guess I can forget about it. If they give me any more trouble, I can always go to the police later."

"Thank you," I say, fighting the impulse to hug him. I think that might make Andrew explode with embarrassment. But the fact that he can forgive people who have been making his life miserable gives me hope that maybe the people I've hurt might be able to forgive me too.

"So, about the dance," says Andrew. "I was wondering what color dress you'll be wearing."

I know I can't put it off any longer. I have to tell him the truth. But then I have an idea. "I'm not sure," I tell him. "If you hold on a minute, though, I'll go find out."

After I leave Andrew's house, I practically run down the street to Marisol's.

"Rachel!" her mom says when she opens the door. "It's so good to see you. Come on in. She's upstairs with Angela." I never really thought Marisol's mom liked me that much, but she seems excited to usher me up the stairs.

When I get to Marisol's room, I can hear laughter inside. Even though the last thing I should be doing is eavesdropping, I can't help pressing my ear against the door.

"Did Rachel really tell you she liked this dress?" I hear Angela say. "It has so many sequins!"

Marisol is quiet for a second. "She said she loved it. Why, do you think she was lying?"

I know they have to be talking about Marisol's sparkly red dress. Of course I wasn't lying. It's gorgeous.

"Probably," says Angela. "I mean, no offense, but it's kind of weird-looking. No one really wears stuff like this. We should go shopping tomorrow and find you some new clothes."

"But I like the way I dress," says Marisol.

"I mean, there's nothing wrong with it," says Angela. "It's just, you know, if you wanted to make more of an effort to fit in."

"Why would I want to do that?"

"You know, so people will like you. So they don't call you Parasol anymore. Now that you're hanging out with me, they're willing to give you a chance, but if you keep dressing like that, no one will want to be friends with you."

There's a long silence. I hold my breath, afraid that Marisol will agree with her. The old Marisol would never do anything just to fit in, but I'm not sure about this new version of her.

"Look," Angela adds, "I'm just trying to help."

"You know what, Angela?" Marisol finally says. "I forgot that I have homework to do. We'll have to hang out another time."

I don't have a chance to jump away from the door before it opens. I peer up at Marisol, probably looking like a guilty cat. She stares at me, her face totally unreadable.

"Hi," I say, straightening up.

"Hi," she answers. I can't tell if she's glad to see me, or if she's trying to turn me to stone with her eyes.

"Hello," says Angela, but we both ignore her. Finally, she lets out a little huff and trots down the hall toward the stairs.

"So, I see you're still spying on people," says Marisol, crossing her arms in front of her chest.

"Only on you," I tell her. "I've decided the spying business isn't really for me."

"So why do I still get to be spied on?" she asks.

"It was only temporary, until I figured out the best way to tell you that I'm sorry." I take a step forward, knowing I need to lay it all out there. If Marisol doesn't forgive me, at least I'll know I tried. "I am so, so, so sorry. I shouldn't have lied to you about Steve and Briana and everything else. And I know you were only trying to help by telling me about Angela cheating. I guess I was just...well, it's hard to have a best friend who's perfect all the time. It makes it really easy to mess up big-time."

I stare at Marisol, waiting for some kind of reaction. Hoping my apology is enough.

She chews on her lip for a minute. Finally, her face softens, and she shakes her head. "Perfect?" she says. "Are you kidding? I've been a total moron the past few weeks. I don't know what I was thinking!" She smiles. "I'm really sorry too."

Relief floods through me. I throw my arms around her and hug her so tight that she actually lets out a little squeak. When I let go, I spot the red dress spread out on Marisol's bed. "I wasn't lying when I said I loved that dress. It's my favorite one. I love all your stuff."

"I know," says Marisol. "Angela's okay, but I think I'd rather have a friend who doesn't care if I'm popular or not."

"You know she's the one who spread the rumor about Mr. Hammond, right?"

Marisol nods and bites her lip. "I'm so sorry I told her. I know you made me promise not to. I was just so mad at you that I wasn't really thinking." She sighs. "And I guess I wasn't thinking when I stayed friends with her after she did that. And after I found out she'd cheated at the bake sale. See what I mean about being a total moron?"

I laugh. "I think it's settled. We were both stupid, but we've both smartened up."

She nods, looking genuinely happy for the first time since our fight. "I hope so."

"Good. I'm glad we're friends again because I have a favor to ask you." I pause. "Actually, I guess I have two."

● ● ●

Once plans with Andrew and Marisol are sorted out for the Spring Dance, Marisol and I leave the Ivanoffs' house and go for a walk around the neighborhood. Even though I'm technically supposed to go back to work, I need this time to talk to her about everything that's happened.

Marisol clucks her tongue at all the right places when

I tell her about Steve and Briana and Caitlin. "I'm going to call Steve tonight and tell him everything," I say. "Hopefully, he'll do the right thing and finally break up with Briana." I can't believe I'm talking about calling Steve Mueller without hyperventilating about it. Things have really changed the past few weeks.

When I tell Marisol about my parents' relationship really being over, she reaches out and gives my hand a squeeze. And when I tell her about what had happened with Evan, she stops walking and gives me a long look.

"You really like him, don't you?" she asks.

I laugh, ready to deny it. But then I realize that I can't. Because I *do* really like him. He's smart and funny and sweet, and he doesn't care about popularity or anything like that. What he does care about is honesty, and I blew it.

"He even said he was starting to like me," I admit. "Before I ruined everything. And now I have no idea how to get him to trust me again."

"Well, someone has to make the first move," says Marisol. "Or you two will wind up not speaking to each other for way too long, just like we did."

"You're right. If I'd just baked you something and brought it over the next day, maybe we would've made up right away." Hmm, that's an idea. It isn't likely to fix everything, but a guy who loves *Pastry Wars* can't say no to a perfectly made dessert, can he?

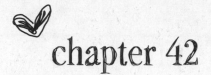

chapter 42

At the end of school on Monday, everyone involved in the bake sale is allowed to leave class a little early to get ready. I rush to the cafeteria so I can make sure everything is set up just right.

Once my brownies are spread out on the table, I glare at Angela who's arranging what look like mocha squares on fancy little plates. I might only have boring old napkins, but I know my brownies are better. I spent hours last night making them, and the house smelled so good that even my mom couldn't stop drooling.

I spot Marisol and Andrew walking toward me, both grinning from ear to ear. "These look amazing!" Marisol says as the two of them come up to my table. "What are they?"

"Banana Nutella swirl brownies," I say.

Marisol squeals and does a little seal clap. "That's perfect!"

"I think they're the best thing I've ever made." I chuckle,

realizing how conceited that sounds. "If I do say so myself. What are you guys doing here? The sale doesn't start for another ten minutes."

"We came to help you get ready," says Andrew.

"I *am* ready."

"Not yet!" Marisol holds up a plastic bag. "I brought an outfit for you to wear. And Andrew has a little surprise for you, something that will bring people over to your table."

Before I can object, Marisol whisks me to the girls' bathroom and herds me into a stall. When I open the plastic bag, I have to laugh as I see the sunny yellow dress from the consignment shop staring back at me.

"I can't believe you did this!" I pull out the dress which Marisol has not only stitched up but also personalized. Now there's a candy pattern embroidered all along the neckline of the dress, though from a distance it just looks like a string of colorful flowers. "It's beautiful," I say as I come out and look at myself in the mirror.

"*You're* beautiful," says Marisol, dabbing a little gloss on my lips.

I don't argue with her because for once I actually do feel beautiful. What's more, I don't mind the fact that people will notice me. If I want my food to stand out, there's no reason I can't let people see me too.

I glance at myself in the mirror one more time, make sure my hair is covering my widow's peak, and adjust my earrings.

"You're wearing the spoons I made you!" Marisol says.

I haven't worn them since our fight, but I dug them out of my jewelry box this morning for good luck. I don't want to ever take them off again.

"Look!" Marisol says, pulling back her hair to show me that she has her spoon earrings in too.

"Did I ever tell you about the challenge I thought up?" I ask. "I think we should have an ice-cream eating contest using nothing but our earrings."

"Ha! You're on, Rachel Lee. Once you win this bake sale, we're going out for ice cream. Now, are you ready to kick Angela's butt?"

"Absolutely."

When we get back to my table, Andrew is just finishing setting up a laptop with a movie playing. As I get closer, I see that it's a silent clip of Marisol in full zombie makeup, ambling toward a plate of brownies. At the bottom of the screen, a caption says: "Brooowwwnies!" And then zombie

Marisol grabs the brownies and smears them all over her zombie face.

"That's incredible!" I choke out, laughing so hard my stomach muscles hurt.

Andrew grins. "I'm glad you like it."

The bell rings, meaning the bake sale is about to start. Marisol gives my arm a squeeze before I rush behind the table, my whole body jiggling with nerves.

Soon people start pouring in, and after that the bake sale passes by in a blur. People seem to love Andrew's film, and more than that, they love the brownies. They all promise to vote for my recipe. Angela's table is hopping just like last year, but I can't help thinking that there seems to be a bigger crowd in front of mine.

At one point, Steve Mueller comes over, grinning at me. "These look great," he says as he hands me money for a couple of brownies. It's nice to take cash from him and not feel slimy about it for once.

"Where's Briana?" I ask. Considering that she helped put together the bake sale fund-raiser, it's strange that I haven't seen her yet. In fact, I don't remember seeing her all day.

Steve swallows a bite of brownie, looking suddenly deflated. "She's not coming," he says. "I broke up with her last night. You were right. She's not the kind of person I want to be with. I didn't think she'd take it so hard, but I guess she didn't come to school today." He gives a little sigh and shrugs before walking away.

After the sale is over, I can barely breathe while Mr. Hammond and another judge count the votes.

"And the winner is…" Mr. Hammond smiles out at the crowd. "Rachel Lee!"

For a second, I think I must have hallucinated him saying my name, but when Marisol shrieks and throws her arms around me, I realize I really am the winner. I did it. I finally did it.

As I go up to accept my award, I feel like I've just been crowned prom queen. Everything is glittery and in slow motion. People are looking at me, but for once they're not laughing at me or calling me a freak. Even Caitlin is standing in the corner looking at me with an expression that's almost friendly.

Once I have a big, fat check in my hands, Marisol pulls me aside. "*Now* can I turn Angela in for cheating?" she whispers.

I glance over at Angela who's throwing her leftover desserts away, clearly furious at how things turned out. I have to admit I feel bad for her.

"No, that's okay," I say.

After all, Angela and I aren't so different. We both wanted to be noticed and respected, and we both did despicable things to try to make that happen.

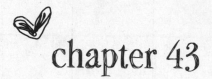

chapter 43

Once I get myself cleaned up after our ice-cream eating contest (which Marisol and I decided was a tie since neither one of us could actually get any ice cream in our mouths), I bike over to the Rileys' house. As I ring the doorbell, I pray Evan will open the door. So, of course, I'm faced with Briana instead.

"What do you want?" she practically snarls.

I swallow, telling myself I won't be scared of cheating, bra-stuffing Briana Riley anymore. "I'm looking for Evan."

"He's not home."

"Oh."

I expect her to slam the door in my face, but instead she puts her hands on her hips and takes a step forward. "So Steve says you're the reason he broke up with me last night."

Oh my goldfish. Didn't Steve know better than to tell her I was involved?

She smiles, her perfect teeth gleaming. "I guess I should thank you. I was going to dump him, but he was so needy. I didn't want him to go all psycho on me. Thanks to you, he finally got a clue and ended it himself."

I can't believe it. After all of that, I actually *helped* Briana? Then I realize that's not true. As much as she's trying to act like Steve breaking up with her doesn't matter, I can see the wounded pride in her eyes. After all, she was upset enough to skip school today.

"Are you just going to stand there?" says Briana, flipping her hair over her shoulder.

I can't help glancing at her chest. It might look real, but it's just as fake as everything else about her. When I look back up, I'm shocked to see her cheeks turning red. I didn't realize her face even knew how to get flushed.

"What are you looking at?" she demands.

"Nothing." Then I can't help smiling as I add, "By the way. Nice bra."

Briana's eyes grow wide, and she staggers backward. The look on her face says it all: she's terrified. Of course, I've already decided I won't say anything to anyone about her secret, but Briana doesn't know that. My smile grows wider and wider. For once, I feel totally in control.

"Who's at the door?" Evan's voice calls from behind Briana.

"Your girlfriend," she spits before storming away.

Evan appears in the doorway, and his face takes on an uncertain look when he sees me.

"These are for you." I hold out the brownies before he can slam the door in my face. "They're peppermint."

He's clearly surprised, but he takes them anyway. "Thanks." He looks under the foil, and I see a smile cross his lips as he catches sight of the frowny face I carefully made out of peppermint candies. "Thank you," he says again.

"Anytime."

"So I heard you won the bake sale competition today," he says. He lowers his voice. "I don't think Briana was too happy about that when Angela called to tell her."

"Yeah, I still can't really believe it."

"I'm sure you deserved it." He shuffles his feet. "So look, I asked Briana about the glass in her room, and she 'fessed up about all the crazy stuff she's been doing to you. I'm sorry you had to deal with that. I don't blame you and your mom for leaving."

"You guys would be better off with a housekeeper anyway."

Evan nods. "We've had a bunch. But they always quit. I wonder why."

We stand awkwardly for a minute, but I know I have to say it, even if it's hard. "I'm really sorry, Evan. I know you think I'm a horrible person for spying on your sister. I only agreed to do it because I was so desperate for money to go visit my dad, but I guess after that it kind of got out of control. I feel really bad about everything. And I swear I'm not a stalker."

"Even though you just showed up on my doorstep?" he says, grinning.

"Good point. The truth is, I'm trying to give stalkers a better name. Don't you think people would like us a lot more if we came with baked goods?"

He laughs. "It seems to be working on me."

We grin at each other for a long moment, just enough time for butterflies to suddenly hatch in my stomach.

"So," says Evan, "there's no way I can eat all these brownies by myself. What do you say, Booger Crap? Want to come in and help me?" I guess that means I'm forgiven.

The stomach butterflies do a happy little flutter dance. "I think that's an excellent idea."

chapter 44

At school the next day, all anyone can talk about is how Steve dumped Briana and asked Caitlin to the Spring Dance instead. I don't hear the word diaper uttered even once. By the time Marisol and I sit down in the cafeteria at lunch, I'm actually starting to feel kind of bad for Briana, especially since she's stuck sitting all alone with Angela Bareli. Caitlin and Steve moved to a different table, along with everyone else who once worshipped at Briana's feet.

"I guess when people had to choose between Briana and Caitlin, they picked the one who isn't pure evil," I say.

"No kidding," says Marisol.

As I peer across the cafeteria, I'm surprised to see Caitlin smiling as Steve whispers something into her ear. Maybe Caitlin will never be Miss Congeniality, but I can live with her being our grade's new queen bee.

"Are you sure you're not upset that Steve's taking Caitlin to the dance?" asks Marisol.

I nod. A few weeks ago, I would have been devastated. But now, I'm fine with it. "Steve's really out of the picture. Trust me."

She smiles. "See, I knew Evan was a way better guy for you!"

"You've never even met him," I say, laughing. Then I catch sight of Andrew Ivanoff walking across the cafeteria. "But maybe we can double date sometime?"

Marisol suddenly becomes very interested in her sandwich.

"May I sit here?" Andrew asks, pointing to the seat next to Marisol.

"Sure!" I answer since Marisol is still acting all embarrassed.

Andrew sets his zombie lunch box on the table and turns to Marisol. "Did you bring the costume sketches we discussed?"

"I did some new ones too," she says, taking out her sketchbook. In a matter of seconds, she and Andrew are having an in-depth discussion that goes over my head.

But I don't mind. It's so great to have Marisol back again. It's like the past few weeks never happened, and our friendship is as strong as ever. In a way, I'm glad things worked out the way they did. Because of our fight, I actually managed to make a couple new friends, something I didn't think was possible, especially considering that a few years ago my dad was my only friend on earth.

Thinking about Dad makes a lump form in my throat. I haven't heard from him since I screamed at him the other day. He doesn't even know about the bake sale. Part of me wonders if it would be better to not have him in my life at all. But I know that won't work. He might have let me down, but he's still my dad.

I push aside my half-eaten lunch, grab my phone, and go hide out in the bathroom. My hands are shaking as I dial his number, but I know I can't hang up.

"Hello?" he says.

Even though I'm still upset with him, it's great to hear his voice. "Hi, Dad."

"Rachel, I'm so glad to hear from you. I wanted to call you, but I was afraid you were still mad at me."

"I am, but I'm getting over it."

"Your mother called me last night. She explained about the plane ticket and everything."

"I'm sorry I lied to you about that. It just seemed like the only way."

"I guess I understand," he says, his voice low and sad. "I just wish I could convince you to come down here anyway. We'd have fun. And you'll be missing out on seeing your favorite show."

"I know, but it'll have to be another time. We really can't afford it right now."

Dad sighs. "You sound just like your mother."

"Well, maybe that's not such a bad thing."

"It's not a bad thing at all," he says. "She's always been the one keeping our family together, despite all my foolish decisions. I want you to know, Rachel, leaving was never about you. It was about a lot of things, but none of them were your fault."

"I know. I just wish you'd talked to me about it first, to both of us."

"You're right," he says. "I should have. And I promise that from now on when there's a problem, I'll tell you. And you promise me too, okay? If something is wrong, you need to talk it out."

"Okay, Dad." I realize how impossible that kind of promise would have been for me to keep even a month ago. I was so afraid of doing or saying the wrong thing that I spent most of my life not doing or saying anything at all.

But that's over now. It doesn't mean I'll never be embarrassed or speechless again, but I'm determined not to let those things control me anymore.

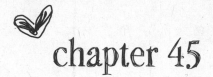

chapter 45

"H oly bean dip, Marisol. You look incredible," I say, helping her pin one last curl into place. She's absolutely glowing in her red dress, and her eyes are sparkling even more than the sequins.

"I hope Andrew likes it," she says, admiring herself in my full-length mirror.

"He'd be crazy not to!"

She smiles and looks at me through her fake eyelashes. "I wish you were going too. I'm so nervous!"

"You sound like me. But you're the one who doesn't get nervous, remember?"

"I know," she says. "It's just that Andrew is so nice. I don't want him to regret taking me to the dance."

"Unless zombies ate his brain, I think he'll be excited."

She beams back at me, and I'm 100 percent sure I did the right thing in fixing Marisol up with Andrew. Not only did the costumes for his film come out great, but now he'll have fun at the dance with Marisol instead of sitting at home because his original date got herself grounded.

"Is your mom still letting Evan come over tonight?" asks Marisol.

I nod, grinning like a fool. "I think she feels guilty that she's going out on a date while I'm stuck here, so she took pity on me."

"Are you okay with her going out? I mean…"

"It's fine." Strangely, it is. Maybe I haven't completely accepted the fact that Mom is dating again, but Mr. Hammond is a nice guy. And he seems to make her happy, way happier than my dad has in a long time. Plus, it's been days since I've had to worry about finding my bookshelves organized by author's last name. That's definitely a good sign. "I'll get over it."

The doorbell rings, and we rush downstairs to open the door. I almost fall over when I see Andrew. His pale hair is slicked back, and he's decked out in a light purple tux.

"You look amazing!" says Marisol. She turns to me, her face glowing. "He got the tux from his dad. It's vintage."

"Wow, it's…incredible," I manage to say without cracking up. He and Marisol will definitely be the most colorful (and most dressed-up) couple at the dance, but I doubt either of them will care.

"Marisol," says Andrew, the tops of his ears red as always, "you're the one who looks amazing."

The two of them look so nervous and happy that I can't help beaming like a proud parent.

"Call me," I mouth to Marisol when they're leaving. She nods as she loops her arm through Andrew's and lets him escort her out to his mom's car.

After they're gone, I grab my journal and flip to the end. *Dirt Diary.* I stare at those words for a minute, knowing it's time to get rid of all the secrets I've been collecting. They just don't feel like my secrets to know anymore.

I tear the pages out, all those words reminding me of how much has changed over the past few weeks. Then I crumple the pages up and throw them in the recycling bin. The minute they're gone, I feel lighter.

"Was that the doorbell?" Mom asks, coming into my bedroom. She looks great. Her bangs are pinned back for once, and she's even put on some makeup. For the first time, I realize that she has a widow's peak just like I do. Maybe no one will ever automatically assume we're mother and daughter, but it's nice to know that we at least have one thing in common.

"Looking good, Mom."

She blushes. "Oh, thank you. I have to admit, I'm a little nervous about my date. The last one was just lunch. But dinner feels more official, you know?" She gives me an apologetic smile. "Sorry, I know this is still a sore topic for you."

It is, but at the same time, it's nice to see Mom looking so happy. "I'll get used to it."

"It sounds like things with you and Evan are going well," she says, putting in her earrings.

Now it's my turn to blush. It's refreshing being able to talk to my mom about things, but dishing about guys with her is going to take some getting used to. "I guess so."

"He seems like a nice boy," she says with a wink.

When Mr. Hammond comes to pick her up a few minutes later, I take a deep breath and grab a plate of brownies from the kitchen counter.

"These are for you," I say, holding them out to him. "My mom said they're your favorite."

Mr. Hammond looks surprised but smiles when he peeks under the foil. "Caramel chip. Thanks, Rachel!"

I wish I could get away without having to say anything else, but this is the last apology I have to make. "I'm sorry about that rumor going around about you. I swear I wasn't the one who spread it, but it was my fault it ever got started."

Mr. Hammond nods. "Your mom told me what happened. I can't say I'm thrilled to have everyone looking at my bottom all the time, but I know you didn't mean it. You're a good kid. Which is why I brought you this." He holds out a *Pastry Wars* cookbook.

"Wow, thanks!" Okay, he's probably just trying to bribe me so he can date my mom, but that's fine. I can't wait to try out some of the recipes. Maybe I can get Evan to help me make one when he comes over later.

"Listen, Rachel," says Mom, exchanging a look with Mr. Hammond. "I was thinking about that class at the bakery this summer. If you're still interested, I'll split the cost with you. That is, if you don't mind using your bake sale winnings to help pay for it."

"Are you serious? But I thought you wanted me to put that money into my college fund."

"Maybe that was a little hasty," Mom says. "Your teacher, Ms. Kennedy, called me the other day. Talking to her reminded me how important cooking is to you." Leave it to Ms. Kennedy to know what to do without me having to say anything. "If you're really going to be a pastry chef one day, taking some classes now will be an investment in your future."

I rush over and wrap my arms around her. "Thanks, Mom." I can't remember the last time I hugged her so tight.

She's beaming when I finally pull away. "We can talk about the details tomorrow." She glances at her watch. "Okay, we have to be off. Have fun with Evan tonight, but don't stay up too late. Remember, we have a long day of work ahead of us tomorrow."

I roll my eyes. "Ugh, I know," I say, acting like I can't think of anything worse. But the truth is, it's just that: an act. Because even if I'll never grow to love inhaling bleach and battling soap scum, I have to admit that I don't hate cleaning houses. Thanks to all that scrubbing and dusting, things have gone from bad to worse to pretty okay. And I have a feeling they might actually stay that way.

Acknowledgments

This is pretty much a list of the usual suspects, but I can never thank them enough.

First, a shout-out to NPR for broadcasting a story about teenage mortification that inspired this novel.

To my wonderful first reader/husband Ray Brierly.

To my amazingly supportive family.

To all my writer and non-writer friends, especially Megan Kudrolli, Heather Kelly, Sarah Chessman, and Alisa Libby.

To superstar editor Aubrey Poole and the team at Sourcebooks for allowing me—even *encouraging* me—to write wacky stories.

To fab agent Ammi-Joan Paquette for her willingness to go along with whatever my muse cooks up.

And to all of you out there who've confirmed my suspicions that middle school is just one big humiliation-fest.

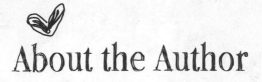

About the Author

Born in Poland and raised in the United States, Anna Staniszewski grew up loving stories in both Polish and English. After studying theater at Sarah Lawrence College, she attended the Center for the Study of Children's Literature at Simmons College. She was named the 2006–

Sedman Photography

2007 Writer-in-Residence at the Boston Public Library and a winner of the 2009 PEN New England Susan P. Bloom Discovery Award. Currently, Anna lives outside of Boston with her husband and their adorably crazy dog, Emma. When she's not writing, Anna spends her time teaching, reading, and *not* cleaning her house. You can visit her at www.annastan.com.

More great reads
by Anna Staniszewski:

My Very UnFairy Tale Life

My Epic Fairy Tale Fail

My Sort of Fairy Tale Ending

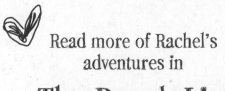

Read more of Rachel's
adventures in

The Prank List

Coming Spring 2014